Lucy Ever After

Heather Cursham

instant apostle

First published in Great Britain in 2017

Instant Apostle
The Barn
1 Watford House Lane
Watford
Herts
WD17 1BJ

Copyright © Heather Cursham 2017

All rights reserved. No portion of this book may be reproduced or transmitted in any form or by any means, electronic or mechanical, including photocopying, recording, or by any information storage and retrieval system, without permission in writing from the publisher.

This is a work of fiction. Names, characters, businesses, places, events and incidents are either the products of the author's imagination or used in a fictitious manner. Any resemblance to actual persons, living or dead, or actual events is purely coincidental.

Every effort has been made to seek permission to use copyright material reproduced in this book. The publisher apologises for those cases where permission might not have been sought and, if notified, will formally seek permission at the earliest opportunity.

The views and opinions expressed in this work are those of the author and do not necessarily reflect the views and opinions of the publisher.

British Library Cataloguing-in-Publication Data

A catalogue record for this book is available from the British Library

This book and all other Instant Apostle books are available from Instant Apostle:
Website: www.instantapostle.com
E-mail: info@instantapostle.com

ISBN 978-1-909728-43-1

Printed in Great Britain

Andrew, thanks for riding the roller coaster with me.

Chapter one

Ella woke with a start. It was that dream again; the third time in as many nights. Each time it began and ended in the same way. She did not understand what it meant, but it must surely mean something. Perhaps she should speak to Lucy.

She lay in bed, impatiently watching the hand of the clock as it climbed slowly from half past six up to seven o'clock. As the time finally aligned itself with her wishes, she left the warmth of her bed and slipped on her dressing gown. For a moment she stood, uncertain, outside her sister's door. When she was little, she used to rush in here every morning, but now she had to knock because Lucy might be getting dressed, and she hated to be interrupted.

Ella tapped gently on the door. There was a muffled reply that sounded like, 'Come in.'

Entering the room, Ella saw that her big sister was still in bed. She must be unwell, she thought. Usually she would be straightening her hair by now.

'What do you want?' asked Lucy, somewhat sleepily.

Ella sat down cross-legged on the carpet while her sister eyed her suspiciously from her pillow. She breathed slowly and considered how to begin. She had a feeling it was not going to go well, but she needed to talk about it, and Lucy was the only obvious choice.

'Before I start, I want you to know that I'm not making this up,' she said quietly.

'Okay – relax!' said Lucy. 'I'm in a good mood; just tell me what you've done.'

'I haven't *done* anything,' sighed Ella, 'I've had a dream. Well, three dreams… What I mean to say is one dream, three times,' she clarified.

'Right,' prompted Lucy, seemingly unperturbed.

Ella relaxed a little. 'Right, so when it starts, I'm always standing in the same courtyard. I look up, and the sky above is the bluest I've ever seen. There's a tower way up high with a purple flag flapping in the breeze.' She paused, and then added, 'I think it's a sea breeze because the air smells salty. Anyway, the courtyard is floored with the most amazing tiles covered in turquoise flowers. Each time, I wander round staring at the floor for ages. There's a window on one of the walls. When I look in I can see an oven with bread baking in it. But it's not like our oven; it's a fire burning in a hole in the wall. I always breathe in deeply, and I can actually smell the fire and the bread! Then, I turn around and notice a well in the middle of the courtyard…'

Ella paused to study her sister's eyes. They were expressionless, but her face had lost a little of its colour.

'Go on,' Lucy whispered.

'So, I go over to the well and there's a bucket. I think about lowering the bucket but just as I'm about to, I hear my name.

'"Ella," a deep voice calls, and my name floats down from somewhere above me. I look up high and notice a barred window in the tower. So then I open a door and climb about 100 steps; round and round they go. I get so out of breath, but then finally I reach the top. Then I'm outside another door.'

She paused again, perhaps for drama's sake, before resuming her account. 'I try the door, but it's locked. It's got a barred window as well. I really want to see inside, so I drag this block of wood over and climb on top. It's really wobbly, but I look in and see this man sitting at a wooden table. He's reading something, but when I call out, he turns and he says, "Ella, you've come! I need you to bring…" How does he know my name? I get such a surprise every time that I start to fall backwards, and I'm just falling into blackness. And then I wake up.'

Ella was still for a moment and her eyes shone, a solitary tear rolling down her cheek. 'I don't know what I'm supposed to bring. I never get to find out.'

Lucy may have looked calm but her emotions were running riot. *She* was the one who had dreams. At least she did when she was nine, Ella's age now. Wasn't Ella just copying her? It even sounded like the Palace in her dream.

'Are you sure you're not making this up?' she asked evenly.

'I knew you wouldn't believe me!' Ella shouted.

She was pulling herself up, regretting she had said anything at all, but Lucy flew out of bed and grabbed her arm.

'Wait!' she urged gently. 'Strangely, I do believe you. Maybe. It's just a shock, that's all. Come and sit next to me.'

As Ella sat down on the bed, she remembered how they would often sit and read books together. She missed those times, now that Lucy had become too grown up for their stories. She waited as her sister dug down into a drawer in her desk and pulled out a tattered notebook. Ella had not seen the book for a long time, but she recognised it immediately. It was Lucy's notes from her dream quest; the one she had experienced years before. Lucy used to show her the pictures and talk about the adventures she had had, and about the boy, Jethro, who had become her friend. It had been their secret; Mum and Dad had not been included. Ella felt her excitement rise as Lucy turned the pages and found the place where she and Jethro had drunk from the well in the courtyard like the one now in her dream.

'The water was so sweet,' Lucy said wistfully. 'I know you're telling the truth, Ella,' she admitted at last, 'because I remember that courtyard. I remember the floor just as you described it, but I never wrote it down, so you couldn't have known. And I remember the window as well, and the oven. But it was cold and black when I saw it. There was no bread baking the day I was there…'

Her voice trailed off. Lucy's dream adventure was the most magical thing she had ever experienced. She wished she could have written more down after it happened. She wished she had been better at describing how things looked and felt. Now it seemed to her more like a distant fairy tale that she had read in a book, or even something she had just imagined.

'But what does it mean?' asked Ella impatiently. 'Why am I dreaming about your palace island?'

'Honestly, I have no idea!' answered Lucy. The momentary snatches of memories of her own dream faded once more and she came back to the present. 'I'm only 15, but my guess is that somehow your subconscious must be playing games with you. Now, hop it! I'm running late and I need to do my hair!'

With that, she gave Ella a little shove in the direction of the door.

'Hey, watch it!' cried Ella, as she hurried out, all the while trying to hold on to her sister's initial response. She had believed her. It was something.

Chapter two

Lucy felt a little off all day. Her sister's dream had unnerved her more than she cared to admit. Did she even believe all that stuff any more? It was six years ago. She had only been nine, and things were different when you were nine – it was fine to believe in magical adventures and dreams at that age. She did not have time for that sort of thing now: she was busy with school; she was getting her own laptop for Christmas; two actual boys had spoken to her today… Life had moved on!

All day she tried to dismiss the nagging thoughts. In her adventure she had been the hero. She had felt full of purpose and so alive. She could still remember the sensation in that courtyard Ella had described. It was like a buzzing inside of her, and a heady drunken happiness that spun her around and made it hard to concentrate…

'Lucy Smith, will you concentrate please! Where are you today?' screeched Mrs Drummond. 'You can read the next page for us!'

Lucy looked around dazed, as a few of her classmates tittered. Daydreaming in the English lesson was a dangerous business.

'Top of page 97. It's a beautiful poem, please do it justice. Read on!' the teacher prompted sharply.

Lucy was very glad when school was over and she could finally go home for the day. Thankfully, Ella did not bring up the subject of the dream again. Lucy was just relieved to be able to put it all behind her and go to bed. Tomorrow would be back to normal, she convinced herself, as she closed her eyes.

When she woke, or at least it seemed to her that she woke, she knew immediately where she was. She was standing in Ella's courtyard, or was it her courtyard – surely one and the same? All the old sensations and smells whirled around her, and the six years that had passed seemed like only a day. The dream had the familiar warmth of the sun, the sharper, richer colours, the elegance, the intoxicating air – even Ella's baking bread. It wrapped itself around her and almost consumed her. Yet somehow she worked to resist its power.

'It's not real; it's just a dream,' she told herself.

Then the word floated down from above: her word, 'Lucy', and she did not even look up to see where it came from. Instead, she walked mechanically to the door of the tower and entered the staircase.

'I don't belong here,' she told herself, as she climbed round and round, up and up. She was warm when she arrived at the door, to be confronted by the barred window Ella had described. Being tall enough, she did not need to climb onto the block. She looked through the bars and watched the figure silently.

He had his back to her. She could still hear her name, spoken by this man's rich, golden tone. His hair was golden too – she could see that much – and he was reading from an enormous book. She did not try the door, only observed him a while, until finally she made a slight noise to alert him to her presence. His chair scraped on the floor as he turned; then he rose and walked towards her.

She felt herself blush. He was handsome, and his blue eyes were locked with hers. Even before he spoke, she knew who it was. Not a man, though almost; it was her old friend Jethro.

'Lucy, you came! I knew you would. You've come to help!'

Lucy felt a great void form in her: a hole, a hesitation. 'Jethro,' she said. His name hung uncomfortably in the air between them. 'I, I don't belong here, I'm sorry I…'

Even before her sentence was complete, she felt herself falling away from the doorway and into the darkness. She grasped wildly at the young man whose eyes shone with hope, but he was gone. She knew what would come next: she would open her eyes and find herself back in her bedroom. She fought the inevitability for a time by keeping her eyes screwed tight, but she could do nothing to block out the tick-tock of the clock. Eventually, she surrendered and opened them. What had she done?

It was early, but she went to Ella's room. Her sister was still asleep, so she sat on the floor, hugging her knees, and waited. She felt awful. But she tried to convince herself she had done the right thing. When Ella woke, she sat up, wide-eyed.

'I didn't have the dream last night!' she said.

'I know. I did,' admitted Lucy meekly. Where to start?

'What? How? Tell me!' Ella trilled, a little too loudly.

'Shh! You'll wake Mum and Dad! I'll tell you, if you'll let me,' Lucy whispered.

When Lucy had finished her account, Ella was horrified. 'It was Jethro, your friend Jethro, and you refused to help him!'

Lucy defended herself as best she could, but it all sounded rather hollow, even to her. Ella was very cross, and black-and-white about it all. He was Lucy's friend; she should have said yes. It was clear that they were not going to agree, and Lucy withdrew. She went back to her room and paced up and down, not knowing what to do with herself. In the end, she got out her quest notebook and looked through its pages.

It had been amazing, she could not deny it, though she usually chose not to think about it. But why would Jethro be locked up? Hadn't she released them from the curse and left everyone to their happy ending? And wait, wasn't it all just a dream?

'Aargh!' she exclaimed, perturbed. 'I can't cope with this! Thank goodness it's Saturday!'

Chapter three

Saturdays were quiet in the Smith household, and they usually ended with a movie and popcorn. Ella had been busy in her bedroom all afternoon and was clearly excited about something. Lucy heard lots of banging and dragging of furniture. At last the suspense got to her, and she peeked into the room. Ella had moved her furniture and put up the girls' tent in the space. There was barely enough room, but she had managed it. Inside, there were two sleeping bags laid out.

'Have you got a friend coming over?' Lucy enquired tentatively; she was unsure whether or not Ella was on speaking terms with her.

'Yes,' said Ella mysteriously.

'Who?' asked Lucy, taking the bait.

'You!' exclaimed Ella triumphantly. 'I've got a plan, to help Jethro.'

'Okay… explain…' responded Lucy warily.

'Well, we need to help him, both of us. I want to come too. So, we go to sleep together in the tent, and then we can both go into the dream.'

Ella was deadly serious, Lucy could tell. She did not want to hurt her feelings, so she spoke softly. 'I'm not sure if it works like that, El, I've never managed to *make* it happen…'

'Yeah, but that was you. I just know this is going to work! Please, will you do it? It's going to work. Will you help me?'

Lucy was struggling with the whole make-believe dilemma. But on the other hand, the look in Jethro's eyes would not let her go. Something shifted in her. 'Tell you what, I'm going to try to have an open mind, and we can give it a go. If we can help Jethro, then we will.'

It sounded ridiculous, saying it out loud, but she was trying to stuff down her cynicism, not to mention swallow her 15-year-old's pride.

'What should we wear to bed?' asked Ella. 'Could we take some tools to help break him out?'

'Hold your horses, little sister! If, and I say *if*, we both end up in dreamland, we don't get to take anything with us, not even our clothes. So, wear your pyjamas to bed like you always do!'

Ella's enthusiasm was not to be dampened, and she persuaded Lucy to agree to a bedtime of nine o' clock. She was adamant that they get on with Jethro's jailbreak as soon as possible. Lucy sighed. What had she got herself into? She had to admit, her little sister was very stubborn, but in a good way.

Ella fidgeted all the way through the movie, and the second the credits began to roll, she hit the off button.

'Come on, Lucy! It's camping time!'

'It's only quarter to nine!' moaned Lucy, but Mum interjected.

'I think it's wonderful what you're doing, Lucy. I only hope you won't be too hot in there together.'

'We'll be fine, Mum!' piped up Ella, pulling on Lucy's sleeve.

'Okay! I'm coming!' Lucy whined. 'Can I at least do my teeth? You never know who you might meet in your dreams!'

Mum laughed as her daughters trooped upstairs. It was lovely to see them spending time together.

The tent was rather warm, as Mum had predicted. Lucy tossed and turned while her sister gently snored beside her. She was tempted to sneak back to her own bed, but then Ella would blame her for the failed mission. She had to stick it out, and then Ella would realise that even if there was something magical, this was not how it worked.

When Lucy finally did fall asleep, it was close to midnight. She found herself immediately back in the courtyard, right next to the well.

It took her a moment to process what had happened. She was back again and had been given another chance to do the right thing. It was not easy to admit to herself, but deep down she knew she had done the wrong thing; but the dream had taken her by surprise, and she had not been ready. She was not sure, even now, if she was really ready. Looking around, she could see the window with the bars on, high up in the tower. There was no sign of Ella. Her sister would be so disappointed, furious maybe! But what could she do? She had tried to tell her that it did not work like that.

Lucy was about to begin the climb up the tower, when she realised that she was going to need something to open the door with – some sort of tool, or better still, a key would be nice. There were doors to three other rooms off the courtyard, and while Lucy considered which to try first, one of them began to open. Before she had time to react, Ella had walked through it and was standing before her, wearing a pretty, pale green dress, and sandals. Lucy's jaw could not help dropping. Ella had made it!

'Don't look so surprised! I've been here ages. What took you so long?'

'I couldn't get to sleep,' Lucy apologised, still slightly in awe of her little sister.

'I've had a look round, and I've found the guard house. We need to get the key, but there are soldiers. But hey, look at you. I think you got the servant costume. Perhaps you can take them some lunch and sneak the key.'

Lucy looked down at herself. She was wearing some sort of scratchy tunic made of brown woven cloth completed by an apron. She even had bare feet. The ornate tiles felt warm and smooth underfoot.

'Wow. How come you get the cool clothes?' Lucy asked. 'Okay, well, let's put together some food, and you can show me the way, I guess. But I still don't get it – I never saw any soldiers when I was here last time.'

They headed for the bakery and peered in the window. No one seemed to be about, so they slipped through the door, drawn to a halt temporarily by the incredible smell of the steaming loaf that sat cooling on the side. Lucy could virtually taste it, and long-lost memories of extraordinary food came rushing up to her. How could she have forgotten? Coming to her senses, she noticed a tray. Quickly, she assembled a rough meal of bread and cheese. She found a jug and filled it from a pitcher, and then she turned to her sister. 'Show me the way, then!'

Ella led her through courtyard after courtyard. It all felt familiar, yet different. There were a few people about. Lucy could see activity behind windows, and here and there they passed a sentry on duty in front of a door. Who was at the top of that tower, Lucy wondered as they passed a fierce-looking man in uniform. He was wearing black, and Lucy's eyes were drawn not to his face, but rather to the golden-stitched emblem on his uniform. It was a peacock's feather, and in the centre of the feather was a creepy, staring eye. She had been feeling perfectly brave until she began to pass the soldiers. Nothing felt right about this, and it dawned on Lucy that there might be genuine peril in their situation. She was consoled only by the fact that no one seemed to pay them any attention.

At that moment Ella turned, and her eyes met Lucy's. They were full of apprehension, but Lucy smiled back reassuringly with more confidence than she actually felt, and they carried on. Suddenly, they were entering another courtyard that Lucy recognised. She had once eaten from the tree in the centre while sitting in the shade of its cloisters. The fruit had been lilac.

'Wait!' she called. 'Let's make the lunch more distracting!'

She put the tray down gently. It was rather heavy and she was glad of the rest. She wiped beads of perspiration from her brow before reaching out to pick some fruit. She placed half a dozen on the tray.

'I wish you were seeing this place under different circumstances, but you mustn't miss out on this taste!' she said to her sister, as she plucked three more and stuffed them into her apron pocket.

'It's just in the next court,' Ella explained. 'I'd better wait here. Just walk diagonally across towards the door to your right. Look confident, like you belong. Find the keys and come straight back!'

'Right.' Lucy picked up the tray and walked resolutely towards her fate, whatever it may be.

Chapter four

The tiles were slate grey in this new space she walked across. It was not a great distance to cover, but with each step the gap seemed to grow, and her dread deepen. She could hear voices: rough-sounding camaraderie mixed with bravado. There was an outburst of laughter as she pushed on the door, doubtless some coarse joke. As the door opened, Lucy felt that her heart would fail her. Surely she would drop the tray and run screaming. The scene played out in her mind, but she resisted it and dragged her gaze from the floor.

Four men sat around a wooden table, playing a game with dice. One of them turned to stare at her. His eyes ranged hungrily over the tray and then settled back upon her. 'Where's Wanda?' he asked gruffly.

'She's sick,' Lucy replied calmly. 'They sent me.'

'Well then, "Me",' said the man sarcastically, 'get on with cutting the bread!'

He returned to the game, leaving Lucy to place the tray on the side. She tried to steady herself as she looked around wildly for a knife. Thankfully, it was lying nearby. She picked it up and did her best to begin hacking at the warm loaf. Her heart was still racing, but she was in the room. As she worked, she glanced to her left, then her right. On the wall opposite was a hook, with a set of keys.

She jumped a little as one of the other men addressed her. 'Hey you, hurry up with that food. I'm starving! Bring it over here!'

Finishing with the knife, she took the tray over to them. They swept their game out of the way as she lowered the food onto the surface.

'Ooh, we get lilacs today!' exclaimed one of them. 'They're my favourite. Wanda never brings us lilacs!'

He grinned crookedly at Lucy, and she lowered her eyes and withdrew. They were greedily attacking their meal, and with a final glance in their direction, she swung by the keys on the wall. Deftly and silently, she lifted them from their hook and slid them into her apron. It was a useful pocket to have, she thought as she left the room and walked away as quickly as she dare.

Back at the lilac fruit tree, Ella was pacing. When she saw her sister approaching, she ran to her. 'Well, did you get the key?'

'Yes, a whole bunch!' she exclaimed. 'Now let's go!'

The walk back to the well felt as if it took twice as long. Lucy imagined every eye upon her, and she counted every footstep, just to keep herself calm. Ella was leading the way, and Lucy kept her eyes fixed on her sister's back. It had never been like this before: the thrill of the adventure, the feeling of being alive. Or had it? Perhaps it had, though the stakes definitely seemed higher now. They pushed on and finally made it back to their starting point.

Ella found herself drawn to the well. Feeling thirsty, she thought she might draw some water. But then Jethro's voice called her name, right on cue. Concerned that the dream was suddenly returning to its familiar path, she turned to her sister. 'I won't slip and fall again, will I? I don't want to wake up yet.'

Lucy was unsure how to respond. 'It's been very different so far, hasn't it? Let's wait and see,' she encouraged.

Together they set off round and round, up and up the stone staircase once more, until they were back at the door. Lucy looked through, and sure enough Jethro was there. 'Don't you ever get tired of reading, Jethro?' she asked lightly.

He spun in his chair and turned to face the voice. 'Lucy! You came back! Ella's brought you!'

'Wait, how did you know it was Ella?'

'She's just like *you*! At first I thought it *was* you, but then I realised your sister must be nine by now. She has your eyes, your hair, even the colour of her dress – she's like your double. Of course I could never forget your face, so I knew it was Ella. And I knew she would bring you.'

'Wow. You and my sister seem to have the same dumb confidence in magic.'

Lucy's words had tumbled carelessly from her lips. As soon as she had said them, she regretted them. It was the same 'dumb confidence' that had got her here in the first place. She was back in the fairy tale. Why was she still fighting it? She could not help it; she was used to doubting.

Jethro looked at her curiously, like he did not know what to make of her words. 'Well, Ella reminds me of you. The Lucy I knew would have leapt at the chance for an adventure,' he said. His words were measured, but soft.

Lucy brushed them aside. There was no time to process this right now: they needed to get the door open. 'I've got the keys,' she countered brightly, pulling the ring of keys out of her apron. 'Which one do you think it is?'

She jangled them in front of the bars and Jethro whistled low, shrugging. 'Trial and error... just get started!' he replied.

'Let me try!' interrupted Ella.

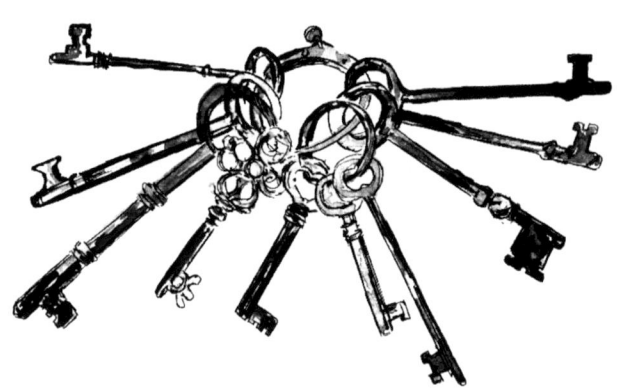

Lucy gladly handed Ella the keys and stepped aside. While her sister was fiddling with the lock, trying key after key, Lucy took a moment to investigate their surroundings. The landing they were standing on had a staircase leading further up. Curious, she began to climb. As it turned out, there were only a dozen or so steps before she reached a dead end. It must be the roof, she surmised. There was a dripping coming down the wall, and the last steps were rather green and slimy. Yuck, she thought, and then suddenly she felt herself slipping, falling into darkness.

When she began to come to, she felt her heart sink. She must be back in her bedroom, though it did not feel exactly like her bed. There was warmth, but there was also movement. And her head hurt. She tried to open her eyes but the brightness burned. She winced and shut them tight, burying her head into his chest. Wait, that was it; she was being carried by Jethro! He was striding quickly, and they were moving through doors and across sun-filled rooms. She was not sure whether to feel embarrassed or just give in to the feeling of safety.

At length, she risked a groan, and Jethro stopped and lowered her carefully to the floor. She opened her eyes cautiously and Ella leant in, providing her with some essential shade. 'Lucy, you're alright!' she smiled. 'You had us worried.'

'I thought I'd woken up,' Lucy confessed, dazed.

Jethro still had an arm around her, but now he withdrew it. 'Bad luck!' he snapped. 'You're still with us.' Then, more kindly, he continued. 'You fell and knocked yourself out. How's the head?'

'No… I'm glad I'm still here…' She sensed she had hurt his feelings. She did not mean to upset him. She rubbed her head and smiled ruefully. 'It's sore, but maybe I had it coming.'

He seemed pacified by her words and patted her awkwardly on the arm. 'Well, Ella got me out, and now I need to get us off this island.'

'On dolphins?' asked Lucy.

'No. That was one-time for me,' he replied firmly.

'What about swimming? Didn't I teach you how to swim?' she teased.

'No, you taught me how to get wet, if you remember correctly. But now, stop talking. I think I preferred you better unconscious.' He grinned. 'The doorway to the King's cottage is heavily guarded, but I found a way out in that archive I was studying. You'll never guess… Can you walk?'

'Yes, I think so,' said Lucy sheepishly.

Ella looked from her sister to Jethro and back. Teenagers were so weird. She took hold of her sister's hand and helped her up. 'I will look after you,' she said importantly.

Jethro led them through a further series of courtyards, and he appeared to have a map in his mind. He never hesitated in his choice of doors, though he was often cautious. He listened for signs of life, but there did not seem to be any soldiers in this part of the Palace. Lucy's head was throbbing, but she tried her best to ignore the pain as the tight grip of Ella's hand pulled her on. Her eyes focused on the tiles of the floor; they were becoming less and less grand, and so she guessed they were travelling towards the outer wall. As a result, she was not too surprised when they arrived at the outermost room next to the enormous drawbridge. She remembered how she had gazed at it from the other side, while sat on the back of a dolphin.

Jethro turned to face the girls. 'This is it: our way out.'

Lucy could not fathom what he meant, yet he turned back towards the drawbridge and kept walking straight up to it. She shot a puzzled look at Ella, who only shrugged in reply. There was nothing for it but to follow, and the younger pulled the elder by the hand until they came to a halt, face to face with the great door. Their noses were almost banging into it.

'What are we looking at?' Lucy asked, confused.

'This!' exclaimed Jethro, his confidence a little confounding.

He put his hand onto the rough wood and pressed firmly on the brass bolt that was exactly in front of him. The girls jumped back squealing, as the ground shuddered beneath them and swallowed a whole stone tile. Jethro nearly fell in, but he pressed himself to the wall before nimbly turning around.

Lucy had a flashback of him, the nine-year-old who was like a mountain goat.

With a flourish, he bowed. 'Your escape route, ladies!'

Ella giggled. Lucy had questions. 'It looks dark down there. Where does it go?'

'You'll see!' Jethro replied, enigmatically.

Lucy had never liked the dark, but she knew she had no option. There were steep steps that led down into the earth, and once they were inside Jethro pulled on a stone, and the doorway closed behind them. The air was warm and stale, and it was now absolutely dark. Lucy thought she had never been more scared in her life. For some reason, Jethro and Ella seemed immune, which was probably just as well.

'It's only a ten-minute walk, maybe 15. I'll go first, let's stay linked – don't let go,' Jethro proposed.

Lucy began to wonder if her waves of panic might drown her. But then Jethro took hold of her hand. His was warm; hers was cold, damp with fear. She gripped on to him as if her life depended on it, and Ella trailed behind, holding her other hand.

They walked, mostly in silence. The ground was smooth underfoot, probably tiled. She could hear her own heart and the breath of each of them. They were heading downwards for a time and then suddenly, joyfully, they started to climb; she felt they must be near their destination. Keeping her eyes shut all the way, she kept telling herself over and over that she was safe.

As quickly as it had begun, it was over. Jethro was pushing upwards through some sort of trapdoor and they found themselves sprawled in a heap on the floor of a small room. Lucy knew it immediately. She had slept in this same dwelling six years earlier. It was exactly as she remembered it.

'It's our hut!' she cried. 'We never knew there was a tunnel underneath the floor!'

'I think perhaps riding on the dolphins suited you better,' Jethro said, pulling himself up and rubbing his bright red hand. Lucy had nearly crushed it in her fear.

'Sorry!' said Lucy, noticing and blushing. 'I hate the dark, you know.'

'I do now,' he replied graciously, with a smile.

'What do we do next?' asked Ella eagerly. She never seemed to tire!

'We'll eat and rest, and then head to my boat. We still have time to make our rendezvous tomorrow at dawn.'

'You have a boat?' Ella marvelled.

'Yes. If we can avoid the patrols, we should be fine. Thanks again, Ella, for coming for me, for bringing your sister.'

'That's okay. Thanks for having me!' Ella replied.

'Anyone would think he invited you to dinner!' laughed Lucy. 'Oh, that reminds me…'

She pulled out the three pieces of fruit.

'I never knew these were called lilacs,' she said, handing them out.

'They're not!' Jethro replied between mouthfuls. 'That's just what THEY call them. We call them *birthday cake fruit*, in honour of a girl who once came to our land.' His voice trailed off, 'If you only understood who you are, Lucy.'

Chapter five

Eventually Ella did tire, and she took a nap on the blanket in the hut. Lucy watched her a while, thinking it must have been how she looked all those years ago. Jethro had lit a fire outside and was waiting for her. Lucy finally quit hiding and went out to join him. 'Okay. Tell me what's happened. Why am I here?' she asked, as she sat down.

He turned to face her; his eyes appeared ablaze in the firelight. 'I guess you're here because you've forgotten,' he suggested.

Lucy tried to digest his answer, but it was not the one she was looking for. 'I don't want a philosophical answer, Jethro. I mean, why were you locked up, why are there soldiers, why isn't the curse dealt with? Why isn't the good stuff happening?'

'Oh that!' he said, playing dumb.

'Yes, that!' she replied, giving him a playful shove.

'Alright,' he responded, becoming more serious. 'Yes, you dealt with the curse. After you left, a tidal wave of good things happened. The King located the resources his father had left him, and he was able to buy back freedom for everyone in slavery. Hope swept like wildfire across the whole kingdom. It was amazing. For almost three years, everything was good. I was studying and helping make plans for schools. Hunger was temporarily forgotten, but we had underestimated our enemy.'

'Your enemy?' Lucy felt a chill despite the fire's warmth.

'Yes, we thought the curse was just the curse. We didn't stop to wonder where it came from, *who* it came from. It just existed, and we just lived with it. Then you came along and broke it. Still, we didn't question why it had started, but then I began researching our history in the annals. Even with all the celebrations around me, I started to have questions, and then finally it all began to make sense. I found these entries, and symbols. Did you notice the peacock's feather?'

'It gave me the shivers,' acknowledged Lucy.

'Well, the enemy is real. They were quite content to sit back and watch us suffer under the curse, but you broke it and that set down a challenge. Their counter-attack has been more explicit. We've been invaded, occupied. Now there is twice the misery and half the freedom.' His tone was bitter. 'We don't know why they're doing it; it just seems to give them pleasure,' he concluded flatly.

'So I shouldn't have done the quest? I made things worse?' asked Lucy, trembling.

'Heavens no!' cried Jethro, taking both her hands in his, his eyes urgently pleading with her own. 'You gave us hope. You gave us a taste of the freedom that is rightfully ours. You won a battle; now we must win the war!'

Lucy was frozen. She pulled her hands from his. He was so brave: She felt like a fraud.

'Jethro. I don't know what to say. I'm not the same person. I'm horrified by what you're telling me. But, a war? I'm only 15. What can *I* do?'

'You're looking at it all wrong, Lucy.' He paused, thinking. 'Do you remember when we first came to these islands? You said something to me that I've never forgotten. You said that I must be there for a reason; I must be perfectly suited to the task. Do you remember?'

'Yes, sort of,' replied Lucy, carefully.

'Well, that's why you're here. Don't worry about what you can do. Just know that you are perfectly suited to the task.'

Lucy closed her eyes. This was too much. She searched her feelings. Everything he said felt true, but it demanded such a leap into the unknown.

Then, in her mind's eye, she saw a butterfly. It was sitting on a flower in a vast meadow, and then it began to fly. It seemed to have no goal in mind, flitting lazily from bloom to bloom. As she watched it, she became the butterfly and felt its carefree peacefulness. Then, in that moment of revelation, the scene changed and the meadow was moving, racing, a blur before her eyes. She was still the butterfly, but she was on her horse, racing to her destiny. With unbridled freedom she let the horse take her wherever he wanted. A feeling like power settled upon her, and she opened her eyes.

The fire was glowing. Jethro was watching her. The magic of this place was soaking into her and softening her as she met her friend's eyes once more.

'You are very persuasive. I am persuaded. I am won.'

Her words sounded odd to her ears, but they were hers. She had spoken them, and it was settled. Jethro smiled broadly.

'I knew you would remember,' he said.

Chapter six

When Ella woke, she sensed that something had changed in her sister. It was as if she had grown taller and even more beautiful. She seemed kinder too – she had hugged her when she woke. Ella could not remember the last time that had happened.

Smoothing out her dress and combing her fingers through her hair, she followed Lucy and Jethro down to the stream to have a drink and eat the orange fruit Jethro had collected for her. Then they all set off for the beach where his boat was hidden. Even though it was dark, the moon was shining brightly, offering more than enough light.

No one had said a word, and she wondered what she had missed. 'You two alright?' she asked suspiciously. 'You didn't have a fight did you?'

'Everyone's fine,' confirmed Lucy, squeezing her sister's hand.

'Here we are!' announced Jethro, dragging some greenery back to reveal a wooden canoe. He began to pull it towards the inky blackness of the sea. 'Hop in, girls!' he invited.

They climbed in, careful not to get too wet. Ella leant into Lucy, and together they felt warm. The sea was perfectly calm as Jethro pushed off and began to row.

'Will you manage?' Lucy asked. Neither of them had slept, and she was not sure how long the adrenalin would keep her going.

'I'm good,' he replied strongly. 'I've been waiting for this day for some time. You get some rest. I'll wake you when we get there.'

Lucy relaxed. Her head did not hurt so much now. She found herself daydreaming of childhood summers. She did not really want to risk falling asleep, but in the end she could not help herself.

It was not Jethro, but Ella, who woke Lucy. Her sister was shaking her wildly, and she wondered if a patrol had come across their small boat. Were they in danger? But then she saw that Ella was in her pyjamas, and she was cocooned in a sleeping bag. She sat up and cried out. 'No! No! No!'

It was so loud that her dad rushed in, with her mum hot on his heels. 'Whatever is the matter?' cried Mum. 'Ella, did you jump on your sister?' she accused.

'No, no, she didn't do anything. I just had a bad dream, that's all. Sorry.'

As her parents disappeared back to their room, Lucy lay perfectly still, staring pensively up at the tent roof. Ella lay beside her. Neither of them spoke for a long time until at last, Ella piped up. 'Why did we wake up Lucy? Why did we leave Jethro?'

Lucy rolled over and stared at her sister, smiling broadly. 'Yes! I didn't imagine it!' she said, very much relieved. 'This changes everything. We need to get back there as soon as we can.'

Ella beamed. 'Fancy camping tonight?'

In the spirit of the sisters getting on so well, Mum allowed them to sleep under canvas for a whole week, but then she put her foot down. 'You have to go back to your own room, Lucy. I'm packing the tent down, sorry.'

'But Mum, you don't understand. It's important.'

'Sorry, enough's enough.'

Ella was glum; Lucy was distraught. It was just not working. Neither of them had had a dream in the week since, and now it was already Saturday again. Lucy's every waking moment had been filled with thoughts of her other world; the one with heroic quests, and the important friendship that made everything around her in this world feel somehow grey and insubstantial. Ella felt it too, she could tell. But they were stuck, and now Mum was taking away their only lifeline.

'Okay,' Lucy agreed diplomatically. 'Just one more night, and then we take it down.' She looked pleadingly at her mum, who sighed and finally agreed.

Lucy felt a small sense of relief, but why would tonight be different from any other?

Neither girl was in the mood for a movie that evening. But Dad had chosen something – he never got to choose usually – so there was no getting out of it. However, from the outset, Lucy and Ella were transfixed. It was not that it was a funny film, or even a particularly good film. But their attention was caught because there was a boy in it who looked just like Jethro. At the beginning of the film he was even rowing a boat across a lake, in somewhere like Canada. And then later on he was scaling a mountain, helping with a rescue – and then he built a fire in a cave. At this point, Lucy and Ella exchanged looks.

'I've got goosebumps,' whispered Ella.

Lucy just nodded. He was just like Jethro, in a cave, or at least it must be his cousin, or some other relative surely. The film carried on. The boy helped with a daring rescue of two mountain climbers and there were other parts to the story, but the girls just kept watching for glimpses of the boy. When it ended, Dad was extremely pleased. 'I knew you'd enjoy my choice, girls. None of your usual sentimental stuff – just some real life and true grit!'

'Yeah, Dad. That was something,' murmured Lucy, 'really something.'

Dad tried to find the usual hint of sarcasm in his older daughter's voice, but he couldn't. 'Well, yes, glad you liked it, like I said.'

'We better get to bed,' said Ella, pulling at Lucy. 'It's getting late for me!'

'I love it that you girls are so into your beds right now,' he chuckled. 'See you in the morning!'

Lucy and Ella were in bed as fast as they could. 'What was that about?' exploded Lucy when they were finally alone in the tent. 'That was so weird. Do you know what I think? I think Jethro's in a cave, waiting for us.'

'But, that wasn't Jethro,' Ella argued.

'Of course it wasn't, but I still say that we're going to see him tonight.'

Ella looked at her sister. She really hoped she was right. She desperately wanted her to be right. A week ago she had had a hard time convincing Lucy of anything, and now here she was, practically unstoppable!

'Night, then,' said Ella.

'Night, see you there!' Lucy promised.

Chapter seven

Lucy was feeling rather frustrated. She could not get to sleep. It was very dark, though she could see the glow of the night-light in the hallway. She wondered what time it was and felt for her watch. It had glow-in-the-dark hands, but she could not feel it, even having checked both wrists just to be sure. Strange – she was certain she had been wearing it.

Then Ella spoke from beside her. 'What time do you call this?' she asked.

'I don't know. I seem to have lost my watch,' Lucy replied, crossly.

'Huh? Well, at least you're finally here. I've waited ages for you!'

'What, do you mean I'm asleep?' Lucy cried as reality dawned on her.

'Sure. Check around you. Does that feel like your bed, or a cave?'

Immediately, Lucy realised that her sister was right. She swiped her arms about until she found her and pulled her in close. 'We did it, Ella! We really did it! So, that's not a night-light up ahead then?'

'No, I think it might be a candle. I've been watching for some time, but I haven't heard any voices, and nobody's come in this direction. It'd be a shame to fall into the enemy camp by accident – we'd better go quietly.'

They stood up slowly. Ella was stiff and cold because she had waited so long for her sister's arrival, but together they began to inch forward towards the light. Lucy was pleased to discover that she had been given a pair of shoes this time, and she wondered idly what her dress was like. This one did not feel scratchy at least.

Finding their footing was difficult, and the floor of the cave was uneven, so the inevitable soon happened. Ella tripped, and as she fell she brought Lucy down with her. They lay in a heap trying to stifle their cries and holding their breath for the longest time as they waited for the charge of some angry guard. But it became clear that nothing was going to happen, so they carried on. The light grew brighter as they neared the end of the tunnel, and they now knew it was not a candle but rather a fire. When at last they ended their awkward journey and rounded the corner, Jethro merely looked up and smiled. He did not seem in the least bit surprised to see them. He was hunched by the fire, and a small girl lay asleep at his feet. At her feet was curled a small, sooty black cat. 'You're here at last. We've waited two nights for you!' he teased.

'How did you know I was… I mean, we're very sorry! I don't think we could've come any earlier! We did try!' Lucy retorted.

'Sorry,' Jethro said, quickly softening his tone, 'your timing is perfect. The children were tired, and it gave us some time to rest.'

'Children?' Lucy asked, not quite understanding. Then, as well as the sleeping girl, she noticed two thin, dirty-faced boys peering at her suspiciously from the shadows.

'Oh, yes. This is Mia,' Jethro said, gesturing towards the little girl, who continued to sleep. 'She's inseparable from her cat, Nightfall.'

The jet-black cat looked up and mewed plaintively.

'I'll get you some fish soon,' Jethro promised.

Then he beckoned in the direction of the boys. They shuffled forward, closer to the flames. Their hair was the same colour as the cat's fur, and their sky-blue eyes sparkled in the firelight. Underneath all the dirt, they looked like carbon copies of one another. Lucy looked closely, trying to decide how this could be.

'These two are twins, Zak and Luka. Don't ask me who's who, they'll never tell you. I'm not sure if *they* even know!' he joked. 'They're about the same age as you, Ella,' he ended.

Ella stepped out from behind her sister and waved shyly.

'And this, boys, is Lucy!'

The twins gasped and looked in awe at the girl they had heard bedtime stories about. Lucy just blushed and hoped no one would notice in the gloom. One of the boys finally plucked up the courage to ask her a question. 'Did you bring your horse, Miss Lucy?' he asked.

'Just call me Lucy, please!' she begged. 'And sadly no, I don't know what's become of Bright Star. He's probably grown old now and eating wild meadow flowers to his heart's content. Now settle down by the fire again, I need to make plans with Jethro.'

Ella moved to sit by the fire, while Lucy pressed on past, towards the mouth of the cave. She stood at its opening and waited. Her dress was the pale blue of a hazy summer sky, contrasting beautifully with the emerging dawn that was casting a pink glow across a landscape of rocky peaks. Jethro came behind her and stood by her side. 'Thank you for coming,' he said. His voice was barely above a whisper, and his words floated out into the pastel air.

'You're welcome,' Lucy replied. 'Now let me hear the plan, but tell me it includes giving those poor children a bath!'

Jethro talked long into the sunrise, filling her in on his recent escapades. 'After our escape from the Palace I made my rendezvous with some of the King's men, and they helped me as far as they could, but we agreed that it would be safer if we separated. I'm heading for a town called Quar, and so I knew it was no coincidence when I stumbled upon my new friends. They were escaping that very place! They were hiding out, and I found them just in time. They adopted me instantly, each one of them, even the cat,' he chuckled. 'I've been keeping them warm and feeding them these past days.'

Jethro's matter-of-fact, modest account made it sound normal. But it was not normal, and Lucy was battling to keep up: his life was so different to hers. They were the same age, yet he had not thought twice about caring for three runaway children! Mia might only have been five or six! Such a responsibility, let alone the life or death context that they were all in. He seemed so grown up and her life so frivolous in comparison. She could not help feeling a little in awe of him.

'But what's in Quar,' she pressed him, 'and why were they running from it?'

'I'm not exactly sure of the answer to either of those questions,' he admitted. 'Quar is occupied by enemy soldiers, I know that much, and I'm hoping they don't yet understand the town's significance either. We need to get there as quickly as we can and find a way to make contact with Mia's grandfather. He has something in his possession that I desperately need to see, something being hidden from the occupying forces. That's what the King told me. It's far too dangerous to leave such a valuable object right under the enemy's nose.'

'But what is it this man is hiding?' interrupted Lucy.

'I don't know,' confessed Jethro, 'but I believe that whatever it might be, it holds some answer to our freedom and our enemy's defeat. That's all I can guess. I only hope we can get there in time.'

Lucy felt the weariness in his words. But then he seemed to shrug it off. 'Let's take everyone down to the lake for that wash you were proposing and I'll get us some fish. We can have a cooked breakfast, and then we'll start the climb down to the plain. What do you think?'

'Perfect,' agreed Lucy.

Chapter eight

Lucy could not really blame the children for resisting the idea of a bath. The lake water was not particularly warm. However, as the sun rose higher in the morning sky, they grew more willing. The boys threw themselves in and emerged shivering, but laughing. Spikes of dark hair stood up and their now clean, identical faces smiled. They warmed themselves by the fire and talked with Ella while Lucy took Mia for her turn. Her matted hair was still full of the dust of her homeland, and Lucy wondered how long it had been since she had washed. She apologised to the little girl before dunking her. Mia gasped as Lucy rubbed her down. To her surprise, the girl's hair emerged a mass of shimmering gold.

'Your hair is beautiful, Mia!' said Lucy as she led the girl back to their temporary home.

'Thank you,' she said shyly. 'Papa says I was given a whole field of wheat on my head. He says to me, "Time to plough the field!" when he wants me to comb it.'

'Your dad sounds just like mine, always making "corny" jokes!' Lucy laughed. But Mia didn't catch her pun. Instead, she replied solemnly. 'Oh no. Papa is my grandfather. My mother and father were killed when I was a baby, and I never knew them. But Papa is wonderful; you will like him.'

Lucy was not sure how to respond to the little girl's revelation and her unassuming bravery. She began to wonder why she had run away, but she let it go. There would be plenty of time for questions later. They had arrived back at the cave entrance and it smelt as though breakfast was ready. One of the twins was diligently turning fish on spits under Jethro's watchful eye.

'There you are!' he said brightly. 'Let's eat! Nightfall has already helped himself, Mia. He said he didn't want his cooked, so I let him go ahead without us!'

After breakfast, they poured water on the fire, and Jethro stamped out the last dying embers. Then he gathered up his belongings and called the little platoon to order. He was holding a small, leather-bound notebook in his hand. 'Right,' he informed them. 'According to my notes, we need to follow the lake shore until we discover the river on the far side. We'll follow it down until we reach the plain, and then we must cross over the Mohr region.'

There was no need for a discussion, and everyone filed out into the brightness of the day. Jethro led the way at first, but it soon became clear that the twins' eagerness was vying for the lead. Mia and her cat were somewhat slower, so before long a natural order established itself. First came Zak; next it was Ella and Luka, then Lucy, Mia and finally Jethro. He was bringing up the rear and carrying the cat. Spirits were high as they walked under cloudless skies beside the curious minty green lake. Jethro explained that its colour had something to do with unusual minerals in the water. He was very knowledgeable these days.

They carried on at a steady pace, and up ahead they could see a grove of pine trees hugging the lake shore. It was the end of the easy, flat beach, and the beginning of more difficult terrain. Still, it had been good while it lasted. The trees came ever closer, and Zak had already reached them. Lucy could see him up ahead. He was leaning against the slender trunk of a tree, looking out across the lake, his eyes shaded by his hand as he stared intently. She turned to follow his gaze but could see nothing but water. Looking back, she saw that he was now waving wildly in their direction.

'Something's wrong!' said Jethro urgently. 'Run!'

He came up quickly behind Lucy and took her hand. He had already scooped Mia into his arm and together they ran hard. Ahead of them, Ella and Luka had disappeared. Throwing themselves into the arms of the trees, they collapsed.

'What is it Zak?' asked Jethro, panting.

'Look, out there,' he replied.

Lucy looked out from behind one of the trees, careful to remain hidden. She saw nothing. 'I don't get it; what are we looking at?' she asked.

Jethro stared patiently from his vantage point and finally exhaled slowly. 'I see it. Well done, Zak! You've saved us again.'

'Saved us?' gasped Ella.

'My brother's got extra strong eyes,' explained Luka. 'He always sees things before me, before *normal* people do!' he laughed, poking his brother in the arm.

'It has its uses,' replied Zak modestly.

Lucy still could not work out what was going on, but finally she saw a dark speck on the horizon of the lake.

'THEY will be looking for *me*,' explained Jethro. 'I'm sorry – I don't want to put any of you in unnecessary danger, but, I'm a wanted man, I guess…'

Lucy wanted to tease him for being melodramatic, but then it did not seem so funny when it was actually true. 'Oh yes, that reminds me, why were you locked up?' she asked instead.

'All in good time,' he replied. 'Let's wait till they get a bit nearer and see what we're up against. Zak, take the others deeper into the trees, and get some rest. Lucy and I will wait a little longer and then come and find you.'

'Okay, will do!' Zak replied dutifully. The younger members headed inland. Lucy found herself a good place to hide, and then began to wait, growing tense as the craft drifted silently in their direction. She could just hear Jethro's breathing in his nearby hiding spot. Finally, the enemy came close enough for Lucy to make out the sound of several voices. Their small craft was blackened, as if it had been charred in a fire, and its sail was also black, adorned with the same feather and the same unnerving eye. There was very little wind, and they were using oars to help with their progress.

'What are we looking for?' whispered Lucy so quietly that she was sure Jethro would not have heard.

The craft rowed beyond their position, and Jethro came behind her and put his hand gently on her shoulder. 'It's just good to know how many of them there are, that sort of thing. That seems to be only a handful of men in a scouting vessel; there must be a larger warship somewhere nearby. Thankfully the enemy is not very subtle, and we have the advantage, as long as we're careful. Come on, let's catch up with the others.'

She could hear the relief in his voice. They were safe for now and soon reunited with the others. The children looked worried, but a smile from their captain set their minds at rest. The enemy was terrible, but they trusted Jethro with their lives.

Zak passed them a flask, and they both took some water. Then it was time to carry on. They would have to break cover from the edge of the trees, but after a short trek they would be in the forest itself. Then they could move more freely without fear of discovery. Zak was sent to scout ahead and find them a way to cross unseen. He came back shortly and reported that the craft had moved out of sight, so they might risk it.

There was nothing for it but to run as fast as they could manage. Jethro was carrying Mia once more as they bolted across the open space. It lasted a whole frantic five minutes, though it felt like so much longer. But they made it, and Zak assured them that he had not caught a single glimpse of the enemy. Setting off once more in earnest, they stayed more closely together for this part, in case they got lost or separated. They wound their way through the dense wood, in and out of tree trunks, trying hard to avoid scratches from the prickly needles of low-hanging branches. To avoid detection from the enemy they tried their best to keep a healthy distance from the shore – near enough that they could maintain their direction, but far enough away that they could not be seen.

Everyone was hungry and tired when they reached the other side of the forest. They had been travelling for several hours, and it had been hard going. Lucy was really impressed with how Mia had kept moving: despite being the youngest she was certainly hardy.

Jethro consulted with Zak and then turned to the others. 'Zak's found the beginning of our river, our way down from this lake, so that we can cut free from being followed. I think we should eat and rest, and then we'll make a start downstream before it starts to get dark.'

Chapter nine

Lucy hadn't given much thought to how they were all going to be fed on this expedition. Thankfully, Jethro had a rough plan. He had always been good at rationing, and this time was no different. While Mia took a nap on Jethro's jacket, everyone else worked to prepare a meal. Luka disappeared off with Ella, returning later with a sack full of berries. Their fingers were stained pink, and Lucy could tell from their faces that they had already enjoyed a private feast. Zak refilled the water flasks, and Jethro produced packets of dried crackers. It was not the biggest meal they had ever eaten, but as Ella pointed out, the berries tasted surprisingly like strawberry ice cream and were perfectly delicious given the circumstances.

'All being well, there might be grilled fish on the menu again later,' Jethro quipped.

Now that everyone was ready to get on with the journey, Zak showed them the way down through the final trees to the edge of a stream.

'I thought we were looking for a river?' asked Lucy.

'It will be. Just you wait and see,' assured Jethro. 'This is how it starts.'

And so they began again. At the end of a whole day of walking, they found themselves beside a roaring, rushing river. There was no way to cross now. What had started as a trickle was now a torrent. They had to shout above its frothy violence just to make themselves heard. Above them, the sun had dipped low, and the sky had faded into a mellow shade of grey.

Lucy slowed her pace so that she could fall into line with Jethro. 'I think we need to stop soon. I know it's downhill, but they must be tired!' she shouted.

He nodded. 'I'll get Zak to find us a spot!' he shouted in reply, and then he jogged ahead to catch the front of the line. Lucy watched him as he described the plan to the boy, and then she saw Zak sprint off ahead. How did he have such energy? she wondered. At his age, she had relied on her horse!

Jethro wandered back up the line. He picked up Mia once more, feeling sorry for her little legs. Lucy offered to carry his bag, but he assured her he was fine. Instead, he passed the cat to her. 'Watch out for his claws!' he shouted above the din.

Lucy stroked the little cat cautiously. Suddenly, Jethro was tugging at her sleeve. She looked up to see that Zak was once more waving wildly. Oh, no, she thought. Not more trouble. But as it turned out, it was the very opposite. Zak had found a woodsman's hut. Ella and Luka were already inside when they caught up. It was basic, but it was shelter for the night, and better still, it had a larder. Someone must have been there recently, because there were jars of dried fruit, beans in a sauce and even packets of crackers like the ones Jethro had.

They closed the door behind them.

'That's better,' exclaimed Lucy. 'Now we can hear ourselves again!'

While Jethro got the stove working, Lucy searched for anything that might be useful to them. 'I've found a couple of blankets,' she called. 'It's a start.'

'I have some more in my pack,' replied Jethro.

Lucy went to pick it up. It was stuffed full, and she tried to carry it to the side of the room that was to be their makeshift bedroom.

'Oh J! It weighs a ton!' she said reproachfully.

He blushed slightly, and then went back to fixing the meal. Everyone agreed that the warm spicy beans really improved a packet of crackers. Lucy could not help notice the quietness around the table, and concluded it was because of tiredness. As soon as dinner was finished, she encouraged the younger members to get under their blankets, ready for sleep. It was Mia who asked Lucy for a bedtime story.

'I suppose I could tell you the story about a boy and a girl who were stranded on a desert island, and all they had with them was a little packet of dried beans.'

'We know this one!' chorused the boys. 'It's a good one!'

Jethro chuckled and hunkered down on the floor next to the boys, ready to relive a little of his boyhood adventure. When Lucy had finished retelling that chapter of the quest, she kissed Mia on the forehead and gave her sister a hug. The twins withdrew to a corner of the room, keen to escape both kiss and hug. Very quickly the room fell to sleep, and Lucy and Jethro sat themselves back at the table.

'Now at last you can tell me why you were locked up in that tower,' Lucy asked in hushed tones.

'Ah yes,' replied Jethro. 'I do have a lot to tell you. Do you remember the King?' he asked.

'Of course!'

'Well, I've spent a great deal of time with him since you left. He is so wise and kind, yet he still seems so mysterious to me. When things took a turn for the worse he grew burdened, yet he was always confident of our final victory. He said he had made provision, and that I must always keep reading and searching until I understood. One particular time, he assured me that there was something to be found, something that would turn the tables on our enemy.'

Jethro fell silent, but Lucy knew he had more to say, so she waited. Eventually, Jethro resumed the story, his voice heavy.

'Then one night he came to me. He was dressed in his bedclothes, with his hair wild. He told me that he might soon be gone. I tried to calm him down, but he wouldn't listen. Instead, he instructed me to leave that very night and break into the Palace. He said that I would know what to do, and he gave me this.'

Jethro put his hand into his pocket and pulled out a small stone. He offered it to Lucy, who turned it thoughtfully in her hands. It was in the shape of a crescent moon and the size of a penny coin.

'It's tiny, what is it?' she asked, returning it.

'It's sort of a key. You'll understand better if I tell you what came next. Some of his men helped me travel to the Isles and I managed to get into the Palace, but I was instantly captured and placed under lock and key in that room in the tower. After a night and a day, I finally began to feel less sorry for myself, and that's when I noticed a curious hole in the brickwork near my bed. It was in the shape of a crescent moon, and sure enough, the stone fitted the hole, and in fact it posted right through. I was sorry to have lost it, but then to my surprise, a section of the brickwork opened. The stone was there inside, but also a book.'

By now Lucy was hanging on his every word. 'Go on,' she encouraged.

'Well, I read it and read it. THEY didn't seem to care. What harm could book reading ever be? I still had my notebook and so, every chance I could, I made notes. I learnt so much from it, not least that you were coming back to me! I also worked out that I needed to get to the walled town of Quar on the desert plain of Mohr. There is something about that place. After my rescue, I ran into the children and could hardly believe where they were from. It was as if they were sent to guide me. Here – I want you to take a look at something for me. You were always better at riddles than me.'

'I'm not sure I'm better at anything than you now,' Lucy replied honestly.

Jethro had produced his leather-bound notebook and was flicking through the pages. When he had reached the part he wanted, he handed it to her. Lucy turned it over in her hand to look at its cover and then glanced through the first few pages. It was full of notations, diagrams and scribblings. The sketch of a peacock's feather with an eye in its centre made her shudder once more.

'Did you do all this?' she asked.

'Yes! It's my life's work – so far!' he laughed modestly.

Lucy turned back to the page in question. The inscription said:

Complete the square, and the eye will no longer see: the desert will laugh, the throne will be true, hearts will unite, and eyes will be lit. Our enemy will scatter and fall away.

It seemed to her a complicated and unrelated set of phrases, and no obvious meaning jumped out at her. 'So you think the King left this for you? I really don't know what it means,' she sighed. 'Not yet anyway. Perhaps it will come to me if I sleep on it.'

'Good idea,' he replied, suddenly looking tired. 'Sleep well!' He grabbed his blanket and headed over towards the twins' corner. Meanwhile, Lucy lay down next to her sister and wrapped herself in her blanket. Jethro's revelations swam about her, and she tried to make sense of the cryptic words, but all she could hear in the end was the river outside, until she fell asleep.

When she woke, she sat up stiffly. Everything was quiet, except of course for the river, which never stopped raging. It had not been the most comfortable night, but not the worst either. Mia and her kitten were asleep, entwined and peaceful, and one of the twins was still buried deep under his blanket. However, there was no sign of Jethro, nor of Ella and, by way of deduction, Luka, since he was the one her sister appeared to have allied herself to.

She began to fold her blanket when the door opened. In walked Jethro. He smiled and offered her his hand. Pulling her up, he whispered a greeting. She could smell the damp, early morning air on his clothing. 'Ella and Luka have gone to collect berries,' he informed her. 'They should be back soon.'

Just then the door opened once more and the berry-pickers rushed in, dramatically slamming the door behind them. Lucy was on the verge of demanding that they show some consideration, when Ella burst into tears and

Luka started talking rapidly. 'We saw THEM! They're camped not far from here. I smelt a campfire, so we crept up close to have a look. They're still asleep, but we hardly have a lead on them. They must be tracking us!'

By now, everyone was awake. The slamming door and the commotion had seen to that. Lucy felt panic rising as Mia joined Ella in crying, and the cat began mewing, alarmed. Thankfully, Jethro was cool-headed. 'Listen everyone,' he said calmly. 'We're going to be safe. I had a scout around earlier, and I found a big old canoe. We can make our getaway by river, and they'll never catch us. We'll be untraceable, but we need to be ready to leave in a few minutes. Boys, you come and help me with the boat. Lucy, you sort out our things.'

With that, he turned on his heels and headed for the door. Luka was right behind him, and his twin was scrambling out of his blanket, his bleariness having vanished in an instant. Lucy packed the bag and dragged it to the door. She also found a sack in the kitchen and loaded the remainder of the foodstuff to take with them. Leaving the cabin behind them, she led the girls down to the pebbled beach at the water's edge.

The noise of the water sent the cat into a mild frenzy, so it was just as well Mia had a firm grip on her pet. To Lucy, the rapids looked angry, a terrifying prospect, and her wide eyes met Jethro's. He deduced their message, but he had no alternative to offer her. 'I don't suppose you have any rope in that pack of yours?' she shouted. If disaster were to strike, at least then they might be able to help each other somehow.

'Brilliant!' he shouted back. Digging down to the bottom of the bag, he extracted a length of cord and quickly tied the end around his waist. Then he wound it round each of them in turn until it came to Lucy, who finished the process so that they were securely chained together. They climbed into the craft, and he explained to them that they must hold onto the rail and never let go. Now there was nothing for it but to push off.

Chapter ten

As soon as the canoe caught the current, it was sucked into a seething mass of white foam as it hurtled downstream. Rocking and lurching wildly, the waters tossed it high then low, drenching them with icy spray. Mia screamed, and Lucy was tempted to join her, but instead she stared ahead, watching with gritted teeth as the ride unfolded.

The early moments of the journey settled into something like monotony, though nothing like a dull groove, rather a constancy of drama. They watched helplessly as the boat lurched past boulders and careened around corners. The most heart-stopping moment came when the river ahead narrowed considerably to pass through a gorge. They were almost crushed against the rocks as they negotiated their way through the entrance. Shortly after, Jethro could see that there was a drop on the horizon. He had just enough time to shout a warning.

'Waterfall! Brace yourself!' he screamed. The canoe tipped over the edge and plunged down what was thankfully only a short drop. As the boat hit the foot and righted itself once more, they were freshly doused with river water. Lucy noticed the cat out of the corner of her eye. He was cowering, drenched, with his claws gripping the bottom of the boat. She would have been more sympathetic, had she not been busy trying to survive the ordeal herself!

At least their descent was rapid, and despite the huge potential for disaster, bit by bit their situation improved as the river became wider and tamer. The gradient flattened, and the landscape changed; their progress slowed right down until they were just drifting. Electric-blue dragonflies flew lazily above the reeds on the riverbanks, and a tranquil lull descended.

'These are the salt marshes,' Zak informed them, breaking the fast from conversation. 'We came here with our father once. We'll soon reach the desert.'

Everyone began to relax; everyone, that is, except the cat. Nightfall was as sulky now as Mia had ever seen him.

'Perhaps when he dries out, he will forgive me,' she sighed.

They untied themselves from the rope and passed around berries and crackers. Jethro began to paddle to speed up their progress, and then the twins took over for a while so that he could rest and eat. Further on, the river narrowed, and its stagnant waters grew clogged with rotting brown reeds. Rowing became harder and harder, and eventually it was clear that they would need to abandon the canoe. Finding a safe place to stop, they climbed out onto the bank.

'What now?' asked Lucy.

'There's an outpost not too far from here,' Zak informed them. 'We could probably spend the night there.'

'Are you sure it'll be safe?' she asked.

'Well, it's very small and out of the way. We can only hope it's been overlooked.'

'Okay, it's worth a try; let's do it. You lead the way Zak!' Jethro decided.

Zak had described it as not too far, but he had miscalculated slightly. In fact, it took them until late afternoon to get near the outpost, by which time Jethro had carried Mia a substantial part of the way. Zak headed off with his brother to take a look round and came back reporting no sign of enemy presence. Placing his confidence in his scouts, Jethro marched his little band boldly up to the front gate. They were met by a white-bearded man whose skin looked as weathered as the old leather boots he wore on his feet. His manner was neither friendly nor unfriendly. 'Good day to you, son,' he said neutrally.

'Hello, Sir. Might we have shelter for the night? We are travelling further into the desert,' Jethro said.

'You're not headed for Quar, are you?' he demanded, suddenly animated. 'It's crawling with THEM; it's not safe for young ones like you, I dare say!'

'Thank you for your warning, but for your safety as well as ours, I'll not tell you the details of our destination,' replied Jethro, somewhat defensively. He regretted the curtness of his tone immediately, but the man seemed to regret his outburst just as much, so that neither fell out with the other.

'Oh, I am sorry,' the man said, retracting his words in a hurry. 'I don't see many visitors here. Please forgive my ill-manners. Of course, you shall have food and shelter, and tomorrow I shall wish you Godspeed, and you can be on your way!'

'Thank you, Sir!' replied Jethro gratefully.

With that, the man took them to the house and left them in the capable hands of his housekeeper. She showed them to their quarters, and they were left to enjoy the accommodation in peace until the next day.

When Lucy rose, she pushed open a wooden shutter to look out on her surroundings. The morning view from her east-facing window was practically monochrome, with a brilliant orange sunrise over a rusty orange sand. It looked like harsh terrain, and she wondered how far they would have to journey in this barren, unyielding part of the Kingdom.

When she stepped out into the compound, she noticed her sister with the twins over on the far side. They were standing in a line with their backs to her, leaning on a crude wooden fence. It looked like a scene from a Western, only there were no horses, for it was the camel enclosure. Inside, eight disgruntled looking beasts were shifting about as much as the space would allow. In truth, they were rather crammed together, a tangled knot of sandy humps.

Just then, Jethro appeared with Mia in tow. He greeted Lucy and then, having surveyed the situation for himself, a funny, triumphant noise escaped his lips. He knew what he must achieve, and so made for his host. The man was hanging back to one side, ready to send the travellers on their way.

'Sir,' said Jethro politely. 'I must thank you for your generosity and kindness in hosting us! I wonder though, how I might persuade you to lend us three of your camels.'

'You can persuade me with money, son. This is my livelihood, you must understand.' His head moved slightly, and his eyebrows rose, emphasising the logic of his answer.

'I've no money,' Jethro responded sadly. Yet he persisted. 'Sir, I implore you, you would be increasing our chances of success so greatly, were you to help us.'

The man looked unmoved and was about to turn away, when something caught his eye. Jethro followed the man's gaze. He was looking in Mia's direction.

'I've always fancied owning a cat,' he began. 'They're very rare in these parts. You can borrow the camels if you will part with the girl's pet. That's fair now, what do you say?'

Jethro's face fell. He could never ask that of Mia. She had been through so much, and the cat was her consolation, her companion: they were connected. It was simply out of the question.

'I'm sorry,' he replied firmly. 'That is quite impossible. We will manage without.'

With that, he strode away from the man, walking towards the others. He had only got halfway when the man called to him. 'You have a deal son, the camels are yours!'

Jethro turned, ready to smile and thank the man, but then he saw that he was holding the cat in his hands. He ran back to confront him, but Mia stepped into the gap and held her hand up to halt him.

'It's okay. I gave him Nightfall. We need the camels.'

'But Mia. You can't give up your cat! It's too high a price!'

'No,' she replied flatly. 'This is important.'

Her face was serene and determined. Jethro was suddenly overwhelmed by the girl's bravery, and he reached down and picked her up, spinning her round and round. 'Mia, you are magnificent!' he cried.

The man was now in a hurry to dispatch them, before anyone could change their mind about the deal he had struck. Mia was permitted to stroke her cat one last time. She whispered words of love to him, and he purred in return. Once the camels were loaded and ready she handed Nightfall over, and Jethro lifted her up, climbing on behind her. Next came the twins on their beast, and on the third, Lucy sat with Ella tucked in front of her. The wind was picking up, and the man gave them a final token of goodwill. Each child was given a colourful scarf to wrap around their head and shoulders – some protection from the sun and the sand.

'Godspeed!' the man called after them, just as he had promised he would.

With the outpost left behind, all around them was whirling sand. The ground was strewn with stones and rocks, all uniform in colour. Here and there sparse vegetation struggled to grow. Gusts of wind propelled them forward, and the camels seemed to know where they were headed so that navigation was unnecessary. A steady train, they plodded on, and nobody wanted to stop. There was nothing to stop for. Being high up on their rides, they ought to have had a good view. But there was nothing much to see, and besides, the visibility was poor and worsening. After many hours, Mia spoke to her companion. 'Look! We're nearly at the oasis. We need to hurry; there's a storm coming. We don't have much time.'

'How do you know, Mia?' asked Jethro.

'I just do,' she replied, matter-of-factly. Then she dug her heel into the camel expertly, as if she had done it 100 times before, and all at once the beast began to gallop. Following suit, the other two began to gallop as well. Ella got such a surprise, she started to laugh.

'What's so funny?' asked Lucy, as the camel bumped across the rocky ground.

'I don't know! It's just funny. This has never happened to me before!' she giggled.

Lucy wrapped an arm around her sister and held on tight to the reins as they raced towards a cluster of palm trees. In no time, they had covered the final distance, and the camels drew to stop in a clearing by an old camel drover's tent. It was there to offer shelter in such eventualities, and they quickly dismounted and dived inside.

Outside the storm increased in volume as the trees thrashed about violently in the wind. Suddenly, there was an unexpected sound. Enormous drops of water splashed the canvas above them, and it lashed with rain.

'That's strange,' said Luka quietly. 'It rained last month.'

Luka was so softly spoken, and the storm so intrusively loud, that his words were hard to hear. Lucy was struck by his unusual comment. 'What do you mean, Luka? It rains all the time where we come from, doesn't it Ella?'

'Not here,' he responded, more clearly. 'Here it rains only once a year!'

Zak and Mia nodded. It was true.

'Hmm,' said Lucy, 'I seem to be a magnet for strange happenings. Perhaps I should investigate!' She strode to the door and pulled back the flap.

'Stop!' cried the twins in unison, but it was too late. They laughed as Lucy drew back inside. She looked like someone had tipped a bucket of water on her.

'We might not get rain very often, but when we do, it's very… er… wetting!' Zak joked.

As time wore on, they realised that there was nothing for it but to bunk down and wait it out. The tent might be a little shabby, but there were enough giant floor cushions to give them all a bed, and it would make for a perfectly comfortable shelter from the storm.

Lucy lay next to Ella, who was trying to fall asleep. 'You're usually good at switching off, El.'

'I know, but I'm too excited.' They were camping out in an oasis, in an exotic, spacious Bedouin tent! It was so much better than camping in the small plasticky one in her bedroom.

'I feel like I'm losing count of the number of nights I've spent away from home, but I don't feel homesick, not for a moment. Is that bad?' Ella asked.

'No. This is pretty amazing,' Lucy agreed.

The rain kept coming down, and eventually they both slept.

Chapter eleven

It was light when they woke, and an eerie silence enveloped them.

'I hope the camels haven't left!' cried Lucy.

Ella and the twins dashed to the door, and pulled it back to reveal the three camels standing still and mute. Everyone sighed, relieved.

'I think we should take them to the well, and water them,' suggested Luka.

Ella and Zak volunteered to help, and so together they led the camels to the well, planning to fill all the water bottles at the same time. Mia stood at the entrance, watching them go. Suddenly, she spun round, her whole countenance full of light.

'What is it, Mia?' Lucy asked.

'Come on. I need to show you something!'

Lucy and Jethro jumped up and set off in pursuit of the little girl, who had already disappeared from sight. She was walking between two palm trees, and they followed as she led them through the trees to the outer edge of the oasis. Just before they reached it, she turned to them and smiled. 'Papa calls this, "the miracle of the desert."'

Lucy moved past her and stood, looking out. It was as if someone had scattered confetti over the whole desert plain. Blossom and blooms of every hue had sprung up, impossibly, from nowhere. They had embroidered themselves into a wonderful rich tapestry. It was unrecognisable. As her eyes drank it all in, she became aware of Jethro coming alongside her. She felt the warmth of his hand closing around hers. Under different circumstances it might have felt awkward, but now it felt right.

They stood in silence for a time and Lucy felt her heart fill. Meanwhile, Jethro had become seized with an idea. 'You know the riddle,' he prompted, rattling it off the top of his head, '"Complete the square, and the eye will no longer see: the desert will laugh, the throne will be true, hearts will unite, and eyes will be lit – then the enemy will scatter?"'

'Hmm,' replied Lucy vaguely, only half listening.

'Well, do you think this qualifies as "the desert laughing"?' he asked her.

'Maybe,' she breathed. 'I don't know. It certainly gives me hope that we might succeed after all. Mia, does it really only rain once a… Mia? Now where's she gone? Come on, J, we need to go.'

Her reverie interrupted, she retrieved her hand and they ran back to the campsite. There did not seem to be anyone around, but drawing near the tent, they heard a girl's laughter. As they opened the door, Mia turned to them, her face beaming. Her cat was weaving its way in and out of her ankles, rubbing himself against her!

'Nightfall has come back to me!' she cried. 'He must have run away and followed us. I hope the man is not too angry.' The little cat purred loudly, happily reunited with his owner, and she scooped him up and stroked him on his favourite spot between his ears.

'That's incredible, Mia. And wonderful!' Jethro added. 'I think this is your reward, for your sacrifice, I mean. Don't worry about the man; we'll compensate him when we can. Nightfall is so clever and loyal to have come such a long way, and through a storm too. He must be very fond of you!'

Mia was so proud she seemed to almost glow.

Everyone was delighted to hear the news of Nightfall's return as they arrived back from their morning work, and soon everything was ready for the final leg of the journey to Quar.

The camels wove their way through the floral carpet that hemmed the oasis. Gradually it grew threadbare until, after an hour's journeying, it was replaced once more by arid rocky land that stretched all about them.

'I think we might have been transported across space, all the way to Mars,' observed Ella at some point. 'Perhaps you can see us through a telescope: three tiny, sand-coloured dots moving slowly across the surface. Except, of course, it's not freezing cold…'

'Huh?' said Lucy, somewhat baffled.

'It's cold on Mars – we learnt about it in school.'

'Ah, so the fact that we are now sweltering tells you that we are not on the planet Mars?' Lucy asked dryly.

'Well, it certainly confirms my suspicion that it's not!' laughed Ella.

Luka turned around when he heard his friend laughing. He waved to her, and she quickly understood his gesture, and fell silent. The sisters watched as the twins increased their pace to come alongside the lead camel. They could not hear the discussion, but they could see Zak pointing in the direction of a steep rise up ahead. As they reached it, both camels came to a halt, and Lucy's obediently followed suit, coming to a standstill alongside them.

'We're here,' Jethro said by way of explanation. 'Apparently, Quar is just over the rise and down in the valley below. We can't carry on without being spotted.'

'Let me show you,' said Zak, and he jumped down. Everyone dismounted and followed as he began to clamber up the sandy slope. Near the top, he fell on to his stomach and began to inch his way forward. Everyone copied him, adopting commando-style tactics to reach the ridge's summit. From this vantage point, they spread themselves out in a line and peeked over.

Below them, in the valley a little way off, they saw the town. It lay compact and secure inside its perimeter, a stone wall that was perhaps as much as ten metres high. The gates were slightly ajar, but there was no sign of life, that is unless you had Zak's eyesight. He assured them that he had counted more than ten guards stationed along the wall.

'Are there any other entrances?' Jethro asked, his voice tense.

'No other gates,' Zak replied, though there are some windows, but they are high up. We couldn't scale the wall, not without help from the inside.'

'It seems we're trying to break into an impregnable fortress, and when we do, the enemy will be waiting,' concluded Jethro miserably.

'We can't give up now,' encouraged Ella. 'You'll think of something, I know you will.'

'Thanks, Ella,' he responded, smiling weakly.

Lucy felt her stomach knot within her. She did not want her courage to fail now, not when her friends needed her most. She felt responsible for her sister's safety, and there was Mia too, of course.

'Hey, where's Mia?' Lucy wondered out loud.

Mia had wriggled backwards and then raced back to the waiting camels. She had collected her cat and was already on her return. They all inched back until they were safely out of sight, before turning to face her. She stood below them on the slope, looking even smaller than she really was. Yet she was striking, with hair that framed her face with gold and her green eyes emitting wild excitement.

'Nightfall will go and get help. I'll send him to Papa and he'll know what to do,' she explained confidently.

Unlike the rest of them, the potential danger seemed to have woken something strong in her. It was perhaps also a result of the proximity of her home. Whatever it was, her demeanour persuaded everyone to trust her.

She stroked the cat to ignite his usual purring, and then, when he seemed quite content, she lifted him up so that his four legs hung down inelegantly, dangling in the air. She looked him in the eye and held his gaze before uttering her command. 'Go home, Nightfall. Go to Papa!'

Then she placed her pet back on the ground. He stood still, tail in the air and back arched, as though he had seen a dog, or had been offended somehow. Lucy's heart sank. The cat was motionless and seemed in no hurry to go anywhere, but then his body relaxed, and he looked up at Mia and mewed. Mia smiled back at him encouragingly, and then quite suddenly, he shot off up the rise and over the edge. Zak raced after him and crouched low.

Everyone else waited patiently for news. After a while, Zak whispered down to them. 'Nightfall is heading straight for Quar!'

There was nothing much to do now except wait. Zak kept watch until the cat disappeared through the main gate, and then he abandoned his post and came down to join the others for food. There was not a huge meal waiting for him, but hopefully they would soon be in Quar, and he was sure there would be more food there. Jethro took over as lookout while the others tried to rest, but without shelter it was uncomfortable.

Appropriately, it was just as night was falling that Nightfall appeared in their midst. With his black coat he was perfectly camouflaged for night work and had arrived unseen. Luka scrambled up the ridge to fetch Jethro down to join everyone as they crowded around Mia. The cat was now in her arms and she, of course, was praising him.

'Look!' said Ella. 'He's wearing a collar!'

Mia turned the collar round until she found what she was looking for. A miniature silver canister was attached to it, and as she unscrewed the cap, a scrap of paper fell out. Jethro picked it up and read it. He could only just make out its message in the gloom, but as he did, he inhaled sharply.

'Well,' asked Lucy impatiently, 'what does it say?'

'We are to proceed anticlockwise to the fifth window from the gate, and wait!'

'I know exactly where that is!' Zak said eagerly. 'We should wait a little longer, until the night is fully black, and then I'll take you. It's a very good thing there's no moon tonight.'

'What about the camels?' asked Ella.

'Don't worry about them,' he replied. 'Mia's grandfather has plenty of men that work for him. They will help us return the camels safely, with ample compensation for the old man. Meanwhile, they'll be safe here.'

They waited impatiently for 20 minutes to drag by before they set off, walking in single file, slowly and silently. They had agreed that there was to be no talking. The journey was fraught under the certain knowledge that enemy guards were up on the wall. Nevertheless, they successfully navigated their way across the rough ground, safely to the foot of the wall. Thankfully, Zak's eyes were excellent for darkness as well as distance, because Jethro could not have identified the five windows they had to count without his help.

They gathered close together at the foot of the darkened window. It was high above them and impossible to reach. As they stood perfectly still, the silence grew deafening. Lucy reached over to find Jethro. She touched his shoulder, hoping that somehow she might communicate, 'What next?' She felt his shrug in reply. The quietness felt like a cage around her, and her sense of powerlessness mounted. Had they made a mistake coming here? Would they stand motionless and mute like the camels until daybreak, only then to be exposed?

Suddenly, Nightfall began to cry. 'Miaow! Miaow!' he mewed plaintively.

Mia tried to quieten him, but he refused and kept his sporadic cry going while they stood altogether, frozen and helpless. Then, just as quickly as he had started, he ceased. A few seconds later, they heard a noise above them. A window latch was being undone! Had the little cat really raised a signal? Now there was a new, rubbing noise. It was the sound of a rope being lowered over a stone window sill. As it reached them, they discovered a basket was attached. Jethro lifted Mia and her cat inside and tugged on the rope. She held on and disappeared upwards. Soon the basket was descending once more. One by one, the children climbed into the basket and were smuggled inside the wall.

When it was Lucy's turn, she found herself rising quickly and smoothly. They must be using some sort of pulley, she thought. Arriving at the window, two arms reached out and pulled her inside. She was dazed, and it was even darker in the room, but as her eyes adjusted, she found her companions huddled together and joined them, waiting for Jethro. He soon appeared, climbed through himself and then helped the stranger pull in the basket. They were inside Quar!

Chapter twelve

Their present relief was tempered with apprehension, for they had placed themselves completely in this stranger's hands. He was yet to speak, but Jethro seemed to understand what was needed. He helped the man stow the rope and pulley inside the basket, stuffing sacking into the top so that it did not look like anything suspicious. After this, the man dragged another pile of sacking into the space between him and the others. Finally, he spoke in a low whisper. 'Everyone, take a sack and get in, and we'll see if we can't get you where you need to be. Who's first?'

Zak volunteered. He climbed into the sack, and the man tied a length of rope around the top.

'Wait!' whispered Jethro. 'Can't I carry one of the sacks with you? I would be too heavy, surely?'

'No, son, it's too dangerous. THEY have an eye for new faces. We must keep you out of sight. Don't you worry, I'm stronger than I look! Everyone, just make sure you curl yourself up as small as you can and try to imagine you're a sack of flour.'

With that, he grabbed the sack containing Zak, and slung it over his back. The door opened, and then closed.

Everyone was rather astonished by this turn of events, but obediently they carefully climbed into their sacks and waited. A few minutes later the door opened, and he was back.

'I've dropped him at the granary, to be delivered shortly!' said the man lightly.

Lucy could not discern the man's expression, but he sounded jovial, and she imagined he was smiling. His relaxed manner was welcome in all the tension. One by one, the children were parcelled up and dispatched to the granary. It was hot and itchy inside the sacks, but no one dared move a muscle. If you peered closely, you could see shadows of detail through the coarse fabric's weave. Lucy chose to keep her eyes shut, but had they been open, she would have seen the stone corridor that was lit by torches at regular intervals. She tried to assemble a picture from the sounds, though, as she was dumped unceremoniously against a wall in the corner of a room.

She could hear people moving around, lifting things, shovelling something, the scraping of a mill wheel. She had never been in a granary, but she imagined the air would be full of dusty white flour, and the floor scattered with wheat. It seemed to be getting warmer in the sack, and she desperately wanted to scratch her nose. How long would they have to wait here?

Finally, she opened her eyes to see what was happening. Peering intently through the mesh, all she could see was a man standing in front of a doorway. He was dressed in black, and embroidered on his jacket was a peacock's feather. The eye looked back at her. She recoiled, though not physically; that would be too perilous. She closed her eyes tightly shut. They were literally right under the enemy's nose!

Just then, a booming voice announced, 'I need six sacks, for the Duke, for the banquet!'

Lucy heard the footsteps, and then she felt herself being swept up and slung over a shoulder. She worked hard to keep her body limp. I am a sack of flour, she told herself repeatedly. Bouncing along on the back of an unfamiliar man, she hoped she would soon be safely reunited with Ella and the others. The wait and the journey felt eternal, but in fact it was only a quarter of an hour that passed.

She heard a door opening and voices, and then she felt herself being lowered onto a soft surface. The next thing she knew, the rope was being untied and the sack fell down around her. Her eyes were blurry, and she rubbed them in the soft, yellow light. When she could focus again, she took a look around. She was surrounded by children falling out of sacks! Their hair was full of static electricity, and they looked as dazed as she, but at least they were all there, and they were all safe!

'Papa!' cried Mia, scrambling out of her sack and running into her grandfather's arms.

An old man folded his arms around her and held her for a long time. Then he looked across to the other children. 'Zak and Luka, welcome home! Thank you for keeping Mia safe!' he said.

This must be the Duke, Lucy thought.

'We had to come back,' Zak began apologetically. 'I'm sorry, but we…'

'Think nothing of it,' he said, cutting the boy short. 'I believe you have done the right thing, for the time being at least,' he added.

Jethro stepped forward to make his introduction. 'Sir, my name is Jethro, and this is…'

'Yes, I know who you are, my brother has told me all about you,' he smiled. 'And this must be Lucy?' he asked, gesturing in her direction.

'Your brother?' asked Jethro, confused.

'Yes, my brother, the King,' he answered vaguely. 'But tell me, who is the sixth member of your party?'

'This is Lucy's sister, Ella. Sir, excuse me, but did I hear rightly? Your brother is the King?'

'Yes, Jethro. You heard correctly. But there is time to talk soon. First, let us get you freshened up, and tell me, are you not hungry?'

'Papa, is there any milk for Nightfall?' Mia asked suddenly.

'Ah, yes, Nightfall. Where is our little furry friend? Surely he is the hero of the hour, is he not? Take him to the kitchens, my darling, and see if you can find him some chicken as well!'

Mia ran off with her cat following fast at her heels. He seemed to understand the word 'chicken'!

'Sir,' said Luka respectfully. 'Are our parents well?'

'Oh, forgive me, boy. I shall send for them shortly! They will be thrilled to see you. But come, let's eat and drink together.'

A servant girl showed Lucy and Ella to a bathroom, where she poured warmed water into a basin and then withdrew. The walls and the floor were covered in mosaic tiles that appeared to depict different parts of the Kingdom. Lucy turned a full circle looking for places she recognised. It was like a map, and it must have taken a skilled craftsman many months to create. Mia's grandfather was an important man. Even under occupation, he seemed to be living well, and everyone treated him with great respect.

Ella was washing her face and trying to smooth down her hair while chattering excitedly. 'Lucy, did you even hear what I said?' she asked

'What? Sorry, no. I was just looking at the walls. What were you saying?'

'I said, I hope I get to go to Luka's house!' she replied.

'Oh, I don't know, El. We'll see.'

Ella moved from the basin so that Lucy could have a turn. There was a bar of soap that smelled like crushed wild meadow flowers, and she decided to strip-wash quickly. When she looked at herself in the polished mirror, she gave a slight cry of alarm.

'I know; you'd never be seen dead like that at home,' smirked her sister.

'Why didn't you tell me? I've just been introduced to some sort of royalty with my hair stood on end and a great smear of dirt across my cheek!'

'Well, there are some fresh clothes laid out over there, so that's something,' Ella replied, trying to sound contrite.

When they had washed and changed, the servant girl led them to the dining room where everyone was gathered. Mia was wearing a fresh dress, and the boys looked respectable as well. Mia's grandfather sat at the head of the table with his granddaughter to his left and Jethro to his right. Lucy found a seat next to him, and Ella slotted in by her sister.

The food was simple, but there was plenty of it: bread and cheese, pies, fruit and cake. It reminded Lucy very much of the meal she had eaten under the King's watchful eye all those years ago at the very start of her quest. Of course, it reminded her too of the first time she had met Jethro. She was especially delighted there was that pink fizzy liquid to drink – the stuff that made you pleasingly dizzy. It was a perfect way to seal the group's friendship and happiness, and in that moment everything past and future was forgotten.

But time never stands still, and the meal was interrupted by the arrival of the twins' parents. This was a joyful interruption, but nevertheless, the moment was gone, and practical things had to start up again.

The twins were going home, but they promised to return in the morning. Mia was tired, and she invited Ella to stay in her room that night. So the girls took their leave and disappeared off, while Mia's grandfather escorted Zak and Luka and their parents out. Lucy and Jethro found themselves suddenly left alone. A comfortable silence descended, and Lucy took another long draft of her fizz.

'You smell nice,' Jethro said, leaning close enough so that his shoulder touched hers.

'That would be the soap,' she said, neatly deflecting his compliment. 'So J,' she said, changing the subject, 'Mia's grandfather seems pretty important, doesn't he?'

Just then, the Duke re-entered the room. His expression was grave. Had his lightness and smiles all been a pretence?

'Now, we three will talk. There is something you must know.'

The change in mood sent a chill through Lucy. She felt Jethro adjusting his posture, as if coming to attention. Yet his hand reached for hers, and she squeezed his in response. They were in this together.

'Mia's in grave danger. I sent her away with the twins so that she might have some chance of safety, but now she is back, right in the middle of it all. I have spent these past years protecting her, and now you must help.'

'But why do THEY care about Mia?' asked Jethro.

'Mia is the King's granddaughter and the heir to the throne,' he replied.

'But how is that possible? Does Mia know?' Lucy asked forcefully, trying to grasp the news.

'No,' he said, a little defensively. 'She knows nothing of this, and for now it must remain our secret. My brother and I have kept our connection in the shadows as much as possible, and I have played the part of her grandfather all this time. I shall continue to do so for as long as she needs my protection. Besides, I am her great uncle, and she is my family too,' he defended.

'Of course we will keep her true identity hidden, Sir. I don't mean to question you – I'm just surprised by your news: Mia – a princess!'

'Thank you,' he responded gratefully, carrying on with his explanation. 'Do you remember when the King's son (my dear nephew) and his wife disappeared? The truth is that they were taken and killed. But the existence of the child was kept a secret, and so far THEY have not guessed. As the heir, Mia is an important symbol of hope should anything happen to my brother. But tell me, what news is there from him?'

'I'm sorry, he didn't give me news for you,' Jethro replied, as his mind flashed back to the last time he saw the King, dressed in bedclothes, with his hair wild. 'He urged me to leave,' Jethro continued. 'He seemed convinced that he was in imminent danger.'

'It is as I feared,' said the Duke, anxiously wringing his hands. 'I feel something has happened to him. News has not reached us here, but perhaps it is only a matter of time. THEY do not know about Mia, but I cannot take any risk with her. She must sit on the throne. I am convinced it is a key part of completing the square.'

'What did you say?' asked Jethro, shocked.

'Completing the square. It is only a legend, but I believe it.'

'We do too!' cried Lucy. 'Show him the book, J!'

Jethro pulled out his notebook and turned to the page where the riddle had been copied out. He handed it over and waited as the Duke read it. His face blanched and then coloured once more, before he finally spoke. He had green eyes, just like his great-niece, and there was a light dancing in them. 'Where did you find this? I read something like this once, many years ago when I was a youth, but then I never saw that book again. It was a great leather-bound tome that I could scarcely lift!'

'I found it, the very same book I'm sure, while I was imprisoned on the Palace Isle,' Jethro explained. 'I think perhaps the King must have hidden it there. He gave me this stone, so that I could unlock it from its hiding place.'

Jethro handed over the little crescent stone. The Duke studied it closely and then jumped to his feet. 'But there is a hole this shape in the wall in one of our bathrooms! I have often wondered what it was for. I thought it was part of the picture, as it is just where the moon should be.'

Immediately, Lucy knew what he was referring to. She had seen it too! Why hadn't she realised sooner? One of the mosaic scenes in the bathroom had a night sky above it. The tiles were dark blue and tiny jewels depicted the stars. The moon was crescent-shaped, but it was not a tile, rather a hole!

'Come! We must discover what my ingenious brother has left for us.' With that he strode out of the room, leaving Lucy and Jethro to scramble after him.

Chapter thirteen

The moon-shaped hole was set into a night sky encrusted with diamonds. Lucy had not realised the extent of the jewels when she had first stood in the bathroom. But looking now across the walls, she could see that many precious gem stones had been worked into the design.

'I thought it might be a map,' she said, as they stood together in the small room. 'Look J, there's the Palace with its two islands, and there's the mountain range where you grew up. The moon seems to be positioned directly above the town we're now in, but I don't recognise some of the other places.'

'That's because you haven't been everywhere yet,' he murmured. 'There's still plenty to explore. But, tell me Sir, what is the origin of this extraordinary piece of art?'

'I believe my father had it commissioned, when my brother and I were still young. We spent much of our childhood here in Quar, and this was my brother's personal bathroom. You guessed correctly, Lucy. It is a map of our kingdom.'

'Shall we see what's hidden behind the moon?' he continued. 'Jethro, I think you should do the honours,' he said, handing the stone back. 'After all, the King entrusted it to you.'

Jethro thanked him and, stepping closer to the wall, posted the little stone through its hole. There was a clunking noise, and then a section of the tiles moved out slightly. It was a piece that depicted some of the wall that surrounded Quar. Jethro dug his fingertips along two of its edges and carefully prised it out until he could slide it. It worked just like a drawer. Lucy held her breath and waited as it slid all the way out into his hands. He turned to face her and the Duke. The drawer was compact and made of dark, polished wood that reminded Lucy of conkers in the autumn.

'For something that is never seen, it's very beautiful,' Lucy remarked.

Carefully, their host lifted out the contents: first, the crescent stone which had had found its way in; next, a sapphire-blue, velvet bag; and finally, a small scroll that had been closed with bottle green sealing wax. The seal had an imprint on it of an ornate crown.

'Why don't you put the drawer back, and then we can take a look at what we've found,' the Duke suggested.

Jethro carefully fitted the drawer back where it belonged until it was once more impossible to guess its existence. They went back to the dining room and sat together with the three objects lying on the table before them.

'I think I should keep the stone,' Jethro said. 'I'm not convinced I've finished with it just yet.'

'I agree,' the old Duke said. 'It's your property. Now that is established, how shall we proceed?'

Even though he was so much older than them, and it was one of his rooms that had yielded the treasure, he deferred to them. They had been sent for this reason, and though he wanted to help, he did not want to interfere. The children were humbled by his attitude, and Jethro proceeded by opening the velvet bag. He loosened its cord and tipped the contents into his hand. There was a ring, delicate and made of rose gold.

'It's the seal,' Lucy said. 'Look, the crown shape in the wax is the same as the pattern in the top of the ring.'

They compared the seal and sure enough, it was a perfect match.

'Have you ever seen this before?' Jethro asked their host.

'Never,' he replied. 'It looks very old and rather too small to fit a King's hand. Try it Jethro.'

Jethro tried to fit it on any of his fingers, but it was no good.

'You try, Lucy,' he suggested. 'Your hands are much slimmer than mine.'

'It's lovely!' Lucy admitted, slipping it on. 'I have got very small hands… but it can't be for me!' she retorted, and removing it, she handed it back.

Next, they came to the scroll. The Duke handed Jethro a butter knife, and he slid it under the seal. After opening it, he spread it out on the table.

'Read it out loud, boy,' the old man prompted, leaning back in his chair.

Jethro looked over the words quickly, before beginning to read. It took the form of a letter:

> To the reader: If you are reading this letter, then times are truly racing towards their conclusion, and you stand on the brink of a very great opportunity. Things may seem dark, and they will grow darker, but you can turn the tide. Breaking the curse has broken you free, but now you must take that freedom and use it. You must finally render the enemy blind and powerless. He might seem to have the upper hand in his occupation, but there is a way to oust him for good. I am writing plainly to you, because you are completing the square and setting everything in order. When all is in its place, the enemy will fall. Protect this ring with your life and see that it delivers you to its rightful owner. I wish that I could have lived to see the day. Godspeed.

When Jethro had finished reading, everyone was silent and thoughtful. Jethro was thinking that it was a hopeful message, but he would have preferred less riddle and more plain text. He worried too whether something terrible had befallen the King. Lucy was wondering about how things might be put into their place. And who was the rightful owner of the ring?

'What do you think, Sir? What are your thoughts?' Jethro asked their host, hoping that the King's brother might have some insight beyond his own.

'Well, certainly, the completion of the square appears to be at the heart of the matter. I believe that as this occurs, something will shift in our favour. I don't understand exactly, but there is a power on our side. I have felt it, and I believe you must have too, to be here, to have come this far. We must trust that we can win.'

'But how are we to complete this square? How are we to understand what the square even is?' asked Lucy, frustrated.

'With that, I cannot help you. You will work it out. But as I said, I strongly believe that Mia is a part of that answer.'

'Perhaps we should take another look at the riddle,' suggested Jethro. 'We need to know what to do next.' His notebook was on the table, and he leant across to pick it up. Suddenly they heard a loud banging and shouting coming from the other room, and the Duke hurried out to investigate. Raised voices continued from next door, and then the servant girl rushed into the room. She looked terrified, and Lucy knew immediately what she was going to say.

'THEY are here. You have to come quickly. Follow me!'

The children jumped up from the table. Jethro stuffed his notebook into his pocket, grabbed the ring and the letter, and ran after the girl. Lucy followed right behind him, wondering wildly how their presence could have been detected so soon.

The girl led them down some stairs and then into a dimly lit room. Ella and Mia were sleeping, but they soon woke and sat up in their beds. 'You must hide yourselves!' the girl said, before closing the door behind them and running back upstairs.

'What's happening?' asked Ella dazed.

'I think the house is being searched,' said Jethro. 'But don't worry, we'll be safe.'

Lucy wondered how he could be so calm, but she realised that they had to be.

'Mia, where can we hide?' she asked.

Mia smiled. 'Papa made me a hiding place. Come!'

The little girl picked up the candle that was flickering on the nightstand and took them to the back of the room. There was a painting on the wall. 'Look!' she said, '"The miracle of the desert!"'

Lucy looked at the desert covered in wild flowers. There it was again. But then Mia pulled on it, and it opened like a door. She climbed in, her candle lighting the way, and the others followed her. Then she bolted it from the inside, so that no one could follow. The room beyond the painting had cushions on the floor, but very little else. Mia placed the candle carefully on the floor near the exit, and then turned to them. 'Now, we wait!' she said.

Lucy felt suddenly drained. Ella was shivering a little, probably from the shock of waking up in the middle of the night, not to mention this more frightening development.

'Come on, El. Come and sit with me,' said Lucy. 'We can keep each other warm.' Lucy sat down among the cushions, and her sister climbed onto her lap. She wrapped her arms around her and sighed.

'It's been a long day. Why don't you go back to sleep?'

Mia lay down on a cushion and shut her eyes, making herself comfortable and looking as if this was a perfectly normal night for her. Jethro, however, was still standing by the door. Alert and listening, he paced back and forth, glancing now and then in Lucy's direction. He looked thoughtful, but mostly weary. Lucy felt her sister's regular breathing and her own eyes struggling to stay open.

Finally, Jethro seemed to reach a decision. He walked over to Lucy and crouched down beside her. He was holding the ring and the letter, now folded neatly to make it small. 'Lucy, I think these will be safer with you. Please look after them,' he whispered urgently.

'But, J, I don't understand. We are safe, together.'

'No, please Lucy,' he urged.

Lucy felt a little sick as a momentary stab of fear pierced her, but then she shrugged it off. They were safe. Of course she would do it, if it made him feel better. So she put out her hand. He slid the ring onto her finger, then placed the letter in her hand, closing her fingers around it. For a brief moment he lingered, his hand wrapped around hers, but then he placed it upon Ella and withdrew. He took up his place by the exit: a sentry on duty. Lucy kept watch with him as long as she could, before falling asleep.

Chapter fourteen

Ella was still in Lucy's arms when she began to stir. She did not feel refreshed as she woke, and was stiff from being in the same position for too long. She wriggled free and then realised something. She was in her sleeping bag. She turned clumsily so that she could see her sister's face. They were back in the tent in her bedroom, and Lucy was sound asleep. Ella did not know what to do. She did not want to wake her, so she lay watching her sleep as dread and disbelief shocked through her.

It was not long before Lucy woke. At first she lay there, smiling at her younger sister.

'She doesn't know,' thought Ella, and a tear rolled down her cheek.

'What's the matter, El?' asked Lucy. 'It's okay, we're safe.'

She tried to reach across to stroke her sister's hair, but her arm was tangled in something, which was confusing, and then she began to realise for herself that something was wrong.

'I know we're safe, Lucy. But what about Luka, and Mia or…' her words faltered. 'We've left them.'

This time Lucy did not utter a sound. The walls of the tent seemed to close in around her, and she felt as if she were barrelling over a waterfall and crashing endlessly downwards. She tried to stop falling, but she couldn't. Then finally she began to understand a little and she reached out to pull Ella in close.

'We'll work something out,' she said. 'Jethro knew we were leaving. He'll explain it to the others.'

They lay together, finding comfort in each other's presence, until eventually Mum came in and unzipped the door of the tent.

'It's late, you two! You've been in there 12 hours. Are you still alive?'

'Yes, Mum, we're alive. We had the best night's sleep ever, didn't we, El?' Lucy's attempt at cheerfulness sounded fake to her, but Mum seemed to swallow it.

'Yes,' replied Ella, even less convincingly.

'Right, well, why don't you go and have breakfast while I pack this thing down? Won't it be lovely to have some space in your room again, Ella?'

'What? No! Mum, you don't understand. You can't!' cried Ella.

'Now, now. We've discussed this. I want you back in your beds tonight. No more bargaining! I really don't understand what's got into you.' With that, she strode out of the room.

Lucy took hold of her sister's hand to get her attention. 'El, I want you to listen,' she began. 'Don't worry about the tent. I know you think you got us there, but you didn't. The tent's not magic. Think about it. We didn't start this thing, and when it's time to go back, we'll go.'

'But how do you know?'

'I just do. I can't explain. I know that Jethro knew we were leaving, and I know that we'll go back again. There is something you *can* do, though…'

'Anything!' said Ella.

'Keep believing that it's real and that it matters,' Lucy replied.

'Oh that's easy,' said her sister earnestly.

The rest of Sunday dragged. It was noticeably quiet in the house. Neither girl felt much like talking. Ella preferred to be alone with her thoughts. After helping Mum pack down the tent and fix her bedroom, she spent the rest of the day at her desk, doing something with paper and pens. Lucy, on the other hand, had a ton of homework to get through, and she buried herself in it, trying not to think about anything at all.

That evening, Ella went to bed at seven o'clock, which baffled her mother, but which Lucy understood perfectly. Not only was her sister hoping to 'get back there', but she was also tired. It had been a very eventful few days! Lucy looked in on her at nine o'clock. She was sleeping peacefully, her hazel-brown hair spread out on the pillow. After watching her for some time, Lucy walked over to Ella's desk, on which lay a piece of paper. She turned it over and saw it was covered in writing. She began to read:

> Dear Luka, I miss you so much already. I need you to know that I would never leave you on purpose. I know you need my help, and I feel terrible. I had the

most fun I've ever had, and it felt so good to be with
you on our adventure. Thank you for teaching me …

Lucy stopped reading and put the letter back on the desk. She was intruding and it was private. Poor El, she thought. She knew how strange it was to go between two worlds, to try to live in different realities all at the same time. It was exciting, of course, but painful too. Perhaps she was getting better at it – or was she? Her way to cope with straddling the two worlds was simply not to think about it. But did that mean she was handling it well? She did not want to dwell on the matter, and besides, it was time for bed.

Unfortunately, sleep was not the escape she had hoped for. She dreamt about Jethro – not that she was back with him, but she could see him. He was in chains in a prison. He had a haunted look in his eyes, and she had never seen him look so dejected. Try as she might, she could not make herself heard when she called to him. It was not a kingdom dream – it was a nightmare. She woke up drenched in sweat, with her heart pounding. It was just a dream, she told herself repeatedly. Eventually she got back to sleep, and when she woke she found that Ella had crawled into bed next to her.

'Hey you,' she said gently. 'When did you arrive?'

'Not long ago. The alarm's going to go off in a minute,' she replied. 'Lucy, I miss Luka. I miss them all.'

'I know; so do I.'

The alarm clock started to rattle and buzz, and Ella reached out to silence it.

'Right,' said Lucy decisively. 'After the night I've had, I need to wash my hair, so I'm off for a shower.'

'At least some things never change,' murmured Ella, vaguely comforted as she climbed out of the warm bed and headed back to her own room.

When Lucy arrived at school later that morning, an enormous banner had been draped across the entrance: *International Awareness Week*. She had forgotten all about it. They were having a week dedicated to world issues. She sighed. She really would have preferred the routine of a normal week!

As she walked into her form room, Mr Atherton was bouncing around, exuding enthusiasm. He used to work for a charity and had spent several years in Africa. He was always trying to drum up interest in 'global issues', so this was right up his street. Lucy kept her head down as he outlined the plans for the week. They were having seminars from different organisations and lots of study groups looking at problems the world was facing. It was all going to end with a mock world summit, where candidates would present their ideas for change. Teachers were going to film students, and the media department were going to produce a documentary.

'The key concept for this week,' said her form teacher, 'is justice. As a form, we will be looking at justice and injustice. I want you all to think about that for me. Specifically, how can we make a difference?'

The bell cut his speech short, and the class filed out. Lucy was off to her first seminar.

Over the next few days, she listened to sad stories, desperate statistics and accounts of natural and man-made disasters. The problems piled higher and higher. Some people were starving; some were eating too much. The rainforest was disappearing; the ice was melting; the skies were being poisoned; the animals were dwindling. There was war, corruption, exploitation, slavery. Now Mr Atherton wanted to know what they were going to do about it all, and he was not joking around: he wanted an answer.

At first the room put forward their half-baked ideas and their hair-brained schemes, but pretty quickly the well ran dry. A general consensus began to form: the world was a terrible place, and there was nothing they could do about it.

Mr Atherton frowned and put down his camera. 'This isn't going to make for encouraging viewing,' he observed. 'What about you Lucy? We haven't heard from you yet?'

Lucy had been listening, but she had not planned to say anything. Now she stood to her feet and tried to ignore the camera. 'Well, I think we're looking at this all wrong. We're far too fixated on the problems, and the more we look at them, the more impossible it all seems.'

'Go on,' said Mr Atherton, his eye on the video feed.

'What we should be asking ourselves is, "What kind of person do I want to be?" There is always something we can do. And if we can find a way to care about someone affected by one of these issues, then we can find a way to help them and fight with them. We just have to realise how free we are. It's the greatest privilege to be part of an adventure like that.'

Lucy had forgotten where she was. She had forgotten that it was not cool to be enthusiastic in class, but she meant what she said. Her life was going to be marked by this, she just knew it. What had Jethro said to her? 'I knew you'd remember,' – that was it. She was not about to forget the significance of her life all over again – she had to maintain her belief in that.

Mr Atherton lowered his camera. 'Wow, Lucy, thanks for that. You really sound like you've walked through this yourself.'

Lucy shrugged. 'It's just something I've been thinking about recently, I guess.'

As she took her seat, Mr Atherton issued an instruction about homework, and with one voice the whole class groaned. They had to write an essay entitled, 'What kind of person do I want to be?' She heard mutterings and grumblings of 'Cheers, Lucy!' from classmates seated around her. Blushing, she began to wish she had never opened her mouth. 'Remember who you are,' she told herself, staring furiously at the graffiti-marked surface of her desk.

In that moment, the bell rang. As if a shockwave had hit, the room erupted with movement and sound. The noise of scraping chairs mixed with the voiced relief for the end of another day filled the room, as everyone poured out of the classroom. Mr Atherton shouted over the chaos. 'Will and Lucy, stay behind please!'

Lucy hung back. Mr Atherton approached her as the last of the students filed out. The boy called Will was dawdling reluctantly at the back of the classroom. He was quiet, and she did not really know him. From what she could remember, he only came to the school last year, and he was from somewhere down south. Finally, he came to stand next to the teacher.

'You know each other, right?' asked Mr Atherton, looking from one to the other. He did not wait for an answer, but carried on. 'Lucy, I want you to speak at the summit tomorrow. I'd like you to work on your speech with Will. I know it's short notice, but I have every confidence in the two of you.'

'But, Sir, what do I speak about?' she asked, nonplussed.

'Just speak from the heart. What you said today, that was a really good start. Will has some insight to help. Trust me, Lucy; you'll be fine. Now off you go, you haven't got long!'

Stunned, Lucy walked out of the room and down the corridor. How had she got herself into this predicament? She had never given a speech in her life. She was happy to be on the sidelines, invisible. Or was she? How was that making the most of her freedom? 'Oh, J,' she mumbled, 'what do I do?'

Chapter fifteen

'Sorry?' said a voice.

Will had been walking alongside her the whole time, and she had not noticed.

'What?' asked Lucy with a start, glancing in his direction.

'You said something,' he said, 'but I couldn't hear you.'

'Did I? I didn't mean to,' she responded vaguely.

'Oh. So… shall we go to the library?' he suggested.

'The library?' She was coming across as really dim – she could not help it.

'The library… to work on the speech!' he prompted. 'Look, if you don't want to, it's fine, but I don't want us to seem completely unprepared tomorrow.'

She could hear a hint of frustration in his tone.

'Oh, gosh, sorry!' she said suddenly. 'I can't. I've got to be home for my sister. She's only nine, and my mum won't be home for a bit.'

'Well, what about after tea? We could meet for coffee on the high street. I could bring my laptop?'

He was making a real effort. She hesitated for a second, then, seeing no way around it, agreed to meet him there at seven o'clock. He wandered off, and she headed home, all the while wondering how all this could possibly have happened.

At the dinner table that evening, Mum had an announcement to make. 'I had a very encouraging email today. You'll never guess who from?'

Nobody tried to guess, and she proceeded to answer her own question. 'It was from Lucy's form teacher, Mr Atherton. Seems he's very impressed with you; he says we should be proud.'

'Well, I'm proud of her,' piped in Ella. 'She's brave and clever and kind!'

'Ella!' scolded Lucy, 'That's enough!'

But Mum was curious as to why Ella was suddenly such a fan of her sister, and Dad wanted to know what she had done to impress her teacher.

Making her feel awkward was something her family had down to a fine art. Even when they were being nice, it felt like teasing.

I don't have time for this, she thought, cringing inside, but eventually, out of exasperation, she answered. 'Dad, I've no idea why the teacher is so excited, but I've got to give a speech tomorrow. I've got to meet up with someone in half an hour to plan it, so please, can we just drop it!'

A few more mouthfuls in silence, and then Mum was back with another question. 'Who are you meeting?'

Of course she had to ask. She had a sixth sense.

'He's called Will. I don't really know him. Mr Atherton linked us up, and we're meeting for coffee, to work. Happy?'

'Nearly. What's he like?' asked Mum mischievously.

'Tall, dark and handsome, if you must know!' Lucy laughed, playing along but simultaneously trying to deflect her mother with a joke. 'Well,' she clarified, 'he definitely has dark hair. He wears glasses, looks clever. I really, honestly, don't know much about him!'

Mum laughed in amusement. 'Okay, no more questions – for now!'

They finished tea, and it was time for Lucy to get going. She got up to leave, and just as she was at the door, her mum called after her. 'Hey, Lucy!'

'Yeah, Mum!'

'We are proud of you,' she teased.

'Thanks!' she replied, somewhat sarcastically, before slamming the door behind her. She could not help smiling as she walked along hurriedly, trying not to be late. She had thrown on her jeans, aiming for the 'not trying too hard' image that she was hoping to cultivate. She had never met a boy for coffee before. Come to think of it, she did not even like coffee, and it was just homework. Even so, she felt nervous as she hurried along.

When she got there, she could see him through the window. He was sitting at a table, tapping away on his laptop. He did look clever. The delicious smell of freshly ground coffee greeted her as she entered. The decor was warm and welcoming, also coffee-coloured, she noticed.

Will looked up and gave her a wave as she approached his table and pulled up a chair. 'What can I get you?' he asked, by way of welcome.

Lucy desperately wanted to like coffee in that moment, so that she could appear older, but in the end she ordered a hot chocolate. He went over to the counter and sorted it out. Meanwhile, Lucy sat at the table, waiting, wondering what on earth they were going to have to talk about. He soon returned, carrying her hot chocolate and his double espresso. Hers was a swirling mountain of chocolate and whipped cream; his, a tiny cup of intensely black liquid.

'A bad habit I picked up in my youth,' he said. 'Cheers!' and he took a sip.

'Aren't you still in your youth?' asked Lucy bluntly.

'I guess,' was his inscrutable reply.

He did not seem in a hurry to elaborate, so she changed tack.

'What are you working on?' she asked, indicating the laptop. She was sipping her drink carefully, trying to avoid the embarrassment of a creamy moustache while simultaneously revelling in its velvety sweetness. She nearly choked on his answer.

'Completing the square,' he replied.

'What did you say?' she asked, spluttering. She grabbed for a napkin, regained her composure, and asked once more. 'Did you say, "completing the square"?'

'Yeah, I'm in the advanced maths set. Its algebra…'

Lucy felt a little disappointed. It was a maths thing, and algebra. She was of the opinion that you should keep the alphabet to English and numbers to maths. Why would you ever want to mix the two? And yet, this was too much of a coincidence, and she did not believe in coincidences, not any more, so she pressed him further. 'Completing the square is maths? I've heard of it, I think. Tell me, what's the idea behind it?'

'Well, it's a way of solving a problem. You have to force things into the right form, and then you can solve it quite simply after that,' he explained, trying not to use too much technical language.

'Show me!' she said enthusiastically.

'Really?' he asked, surprised. Nevertheless, he ran through a couple of problems on the screen, until her eyes began to glaze over. She sat back, frowning.

'Sorry to bore you,' he said defensively.

'No, I'm concentrating, honestly!' she said.

He gulped down his coffee and sat eyeing her suspiciously. His fair assumption was that she was making fun of him, and he could not help feeling cross with Mr Atherton for having dropped him in it. 'Look, if you don't want to be here…'

Lucy was frustrated. She was making a mess of things. She would have to think about the maths riddle later.

'I'm sorry! Genuinely! I was trying to understand, really. It's just that maths isn't my strength. But maybe we should get on with this speech. I'm not even sure what I'm meant to be doing.'

Will relaxed a little. Lucy seemed to be telling the truth. 'Mr A has emailed me. He wants you to do the closing remarks. He wants you to finish the whole thing off with your ideas. I did like what you said, by the way – that is, if you meant it.'

'Of course I meant it. I just don't know if I can do it again, in front of lots of people,' she said uncertainly. Then she continued. 'So what advice do you have? Why did Sir pick you?'

'He knows my parents,' he admitted. 'They spent time together in Africa, before I was born. They're missionaries. I lived there all my life, until we moved back here last year. The government had to get us out; we got caught up in a coup.'

'What do you mean?'

'Well, my parents helped set up a hospital and a school in a town in the Congo. There were rumours of the army taking over. In the end, the government arranged for our transport out. They said it was "not safe" for us.' He spoke this last phrase with some bitterness. 'It wasn't safe for the children in our school either. I don't suppose you've ever seen armed soldiers on the streets; it's such an outrageous wrong.'

Will's words sounded angry, but he looked weary. He looked nothing like Jethro, and yet he had Jethro's look in his eyes, and Lucy forgot that they had only just met. Her heart went out to him, and she reached out a hand to touch his.

'Will, that's terrible. I'm so sorry,' she said softly. 'I know how hard it is to leave people behind, in danger.'

'You do?' he asked, momentarily vulnerable.

Lucy sat back, thinking. She couldn't explain herself. She'd sound crazy, but she was telling the truth.

'Yes, I do,' she said. 'And I think they understand that you did what you could,' she concluded. 'Now, let's write a speech, for the people who need our help.'

It was dark outside when they finished working. Will closed his laptop, promising to print the document and bring it in the morning. 'I'll walk you home,' he offered.

They were quiet as they walked along. Lucy wished she knew Will better, that she could talk to him openly and be herself. Maybe that would come. She already felt more comfortable.

'This is me,' she said, when they got near her house. 'Thanks for helping and er, thanks for talking to me, about you, I mean.'

'Next time, maybe, we'll talk about you,' he replied.

'Next time… sounds good,' she concluded. 'See you tomorrow.'

When she got through the front door, Mum was waiting.

'How was tall, dark and handsome?' she asked, pouncing on her daughter before she could get past.

'Interesting, unexpected, nice accent – soft vowels. Oh, and none of your business of course, Mother!'

'Of course!' said Mum, smiling. 'Now off to bed; you've got a big day tomorrow!'

'Don't remind me,' groaned Lucy, heading for the stairs.

Chapter sixteen

The surprising thing about the summit, apart from being much better than anyone expected, was the speech made by Will. Lucy did not even know he was giving one. He had certainly never let on that he was. They had not had much opportunity to speak together that day, since he had merely delivered the notes to her desk that morning. Later, she had seen him deep in conversation with Mr Atherton, but after that they had had no classes together. They had been allocated adjacent seats at the summit. She was fidgeting nervously, but he was perfectly still.

The other candidates did a good job outlining their findings and describing work that was underway to help address the various crises. Then Mr Atherton asked Will to come out, introducing him in glowing terms, as a hero; someone with first-hand knowledge to share. The room fell silent, all eyes on Will.

'Thank you,' he began. 'But I'm not a hero. Sometimes you find yourself in a situation, and you just do what you have to, because you can help. Almost every day, we have opportunities to help out, and maybe my story sounds exciting, but I just happened to be there, and people that I consider my friends needed me, so I did what I could. My friends are growing up in a dangerous part of the world; their lives are a struggle.'

Will went on to describe a night when he had fled from soldiers with a group of children from the school. They had spent the night in hiding, not knowing if their families were safe. Lucy could not help but be transported by her imagination as he described the darkness, the sounds, the smells. The account spilled out vividly from his memory, and momentarily the whole room found themselves running scared from a hostile threat under a vast starry sky.

'But the surprising thing I found,' he said, 'was the hope. It's not that the children weren't frightened; they were. But they were so confident and grateful and hopeful. Every day I regret being pulled out, but I think perhaps they understand.' At this point he glanced briefly in Lucy's direction, before concluding. 'I know it won't be the last time I find myself in a situation like that. I know that I must live a life that is worthy. I can't just offer my sympathy – I have to offer myself.'

Everyone applauded as he went to take his seat. He did not enjoy the attention and ducked down as quickly as he could.

'That was amazing!' Lucy said above the noise. 'Is that where you left your youth behind – in the darkness, that night?'

He looked at her, surprised. 'Something like that,' he said, touched by her sensitivity. Then, with an encouraging smile, he urged her to the front, 'Your turn!'

Lucy walked to the lectern, paper in hand. She glanced at the notes, but she did not really need them. Now that it came to it, she knew what she wanted to say.

'Someone wise once told me I had a choice. Life could pass me by, or if I was willing, life could be the adventure it was meant to be. I want to present us all with a challenge today. Are you willing to take the risk? We've all heard Will's story. He chose to take a risk, and I think we are left in no doubt: he does not regret it for a moment.

'We can let the difficulties stare us in the face, intimidate us, confuse us, even overwhelm us. Or we can rise to the challenge. I'm not saying it won't be hard or costly, but it's so worth it. I believe there is an adventure waiting for every one of us. Here I am, ready to meet my life head-on. "Send me!" I say. What do you say?'

With that, she sat down. Mr Atherton rushed over to the lectern.

'Wow!' he said, smiling out at the school. 'What a brilliant way to end the week! The ball's in our court, school. What are we going to do?'

The summit was at an end, and everyone was free to go. Mr Atherton managed to catch Lucy before she had a chance to leave. 'You two were perfect!' he said, putting an affectionate arm around Will. 'I know that wasn't easy for you, Will, but it really helps people to understand. And Lucy – I knew you two would work well together – Will could really do with a good friend!'

Will pulled out from the teacher's side hug, having turned the colour of ripe tomatoes. 'Really Mr A! You had to go there! You're worse than Dad…' However, rather than angry, he sounded amused.

'Lucy, I apologise!' said Mr Atherton, but he, too, was clearly still joking around.

This was a side of her teacher she had never been privy to! She felt a bit awkward, like she was intruding on family, but then at the same time she felt welcomed in, so she went with it. 'Will, I think we should go!' she said, taking mock offence.

'Yes, let's get out of here!' he said, laughing. In a moment of giddy recklessness, he took her hand and swept her out of the teacher's presence towards the exit. As they left the lecture hall, they came to their senses, almost strangers once more. He let go of her hand.

'Sorry,' he said awkwardly.

'Perhaps we can put it down to post-speech madness?' Lucy suggested kindly. 'Or too much coffee?'

'I'll never hear the end of it,' he said ruefully, then more quietly and more to himself, 'Oh well, it was worth it.'

Lucy was not sure how to react.

'Listen, I need to go. I've got to get back for…'

'… your sister,' he said, finishing her sentence. 'I know.'

'Okay. Well, you did great… I'll see you soon.' Lucy smiled goodbye and began to walk away.

'Wait!' he called after her.

She stopped and turned to look back.

'Mr A was right,' he confessed, then hesitated. 'You know, about me needing a friend.'

He looked shy and beautiful to her in that moment, but she did not have a bold answer. Instead, she mirrored his shyness. 'I'll have to think about it,' she replied lightly, but she smiled to herself as she left.

Ella was late out of school, and Lucy waited in the playground, hoping that the rain would hold off. Her thoughts drifted between Jethro and Will. They seemed more and more connected: unlikely heroes, yet brave and full of heart. They would like each other, she thought, though it might be a little complicated. She was still smiling to herself mischievously when, finally, her sister appeared. She was looking decidedly unhappy.

'What's up?' Lucy asked her, as they hurried home under the angry sky.

'Nothing,' said Ella crossly.

It started to rain, lightly.

'Come on – you can tell me,' Lucy coaxed her.

'Well,' her sister relented, 'I told Amelia about the dream, because I thought she was my friend, and she laughed at me. She was really mean to me all day, and she told Millie and Jess, and now they all think I'm weird.'

'Oh, El. I'm sorry! I guess it's not the kind of thing you can share with just anybody. But just because someone won't believe you, that doesn't mean they're right. We have to hold on to that, okay?'

'Okay,' agreed Ella, looking more cheerful, but also more bedraggled.

The rain was getting heavier, and suddenly it began to really bucket down. The girls shrieked in dismay but then surrendered, laughing as they ran the rest of the way home.

After she had changed into dry clothes, Lucy sat down at the computer. There were some things she wanted to research – completing the square, for one. Try as she might, though, it made no sense. Next, she read up on flowering deserts. This was more interesting. There was a really spectacular example in Chile. It did not happen every year, only in years where there were unusual amounts of rain. It certainly did not happen overnight, like it had for them. What they had witnessed was marvellous, perhaps even miraculous, but then the laws of nature did seem to operate with more flexibility in the Kingdom.

She sat back, thinking. Why were riddles so hard to understand? They were messy, non-linear, like colouring outside the lines. Perhaps if she could put all the ingredients in a bottle and shake them together, something would fall out. Amused by this idea, she drew a bottle and started to draw things inside. There was a heart, some hands, a ring, a moon-shaped stone, Mia, a square, flowers, Jethro, the twins, Ella, herself. She imagined them all thrown together and shaken around.

Just then, Ella came into the room. 'What's this?' she asked.

Lucy tried to explain as best she could. Ella took another good look. Then, suddenly inspired, she took the pen from her sister and drew her own rough sketch.

'Hmm. Well, a square has four sides. So you would have Mia on one side, Jethro on the next, with Zak and Luka on the other two. Then you could put the flowers and the ring with Mia, because she's a princess. Give the stone to Jethro, because it's his. Then, er, well, they could all hold hands, and I will put the heart right around all of them. There,' she said, satisfied.

'What about us?' Lucy asked, feeling strangely unnerved.

'Well, *we* have to get them organised. You know, get them together, as the square, inside the heart?'

'Ella, you're amazing. How did you do that?'

'What? I was joking. I made it up, silly!'

But Lucy was experiencing that feeling she got when she knew that she knew something. It felt like tingling, butterflies and goosebumps all at once.

'When you complete the square, "you force something to fit into the right form to make it easy to solve"!' she said excitedly, recalling Will's advice. 'We have to get the sides of the square together, you and me! But, we have to tell Jethro! Ella, you're a genius.'

Ella had no idea what her sister was getting at, but she was happy to have helped. She shrugged and walked out again. Lucy was excitedly pacing up and down when her mum arrived home. In fact, she was still pacing up and down when her dad came home. And as soon as tea was over, she paced up and down some more.

'Will you please sit down, Lucy, or find something to do. What on earth has got you so fired up?' Mum asked her.

'What?' she asked distractedly. 'Oh, nothing. It's nothing.'

She took herself off to her room. Perhaps if she read a book it would take her mind off things. It would need to be a good book, though, she thought. There was that book she had taken out of the library – the one that had won a prize.

She stretched out on the bed and tried to relax. Opening to page one, she began to read. It was about a girl a bit younger than her, who was sent to South America to live with some distant relatives. The book was perhaps a little young for her, but that made it a joy to read, because it was easy for her to race through, yet beautifully written, so she could stop and appreciate the language as she read.

The heroine found herself placed with a truly horrid family, but made a wonderful friend, and they would sneak out together, escaping into the Amazonian jungle to explore its wonders. She would have to encourage Ella to read it, she thought, as she yawned. As she read on about their drama in the rainforest, it became more and more real to her, until it was almost as though she herself were walking through the warm, steamy greenery, wiping her brow, listening to the chorus of tropical birds…

Chapter seventeen

Ella was off to bed. She looked in on Lucy, wondering if she was still pacing or whether she had finally calmed down. Of course, she could understand her sister's frustration, but Lucy herself had said that they should be patient. She was not setting a good example!

However, Lucy was not pacing. She was lying on her bed, fully dressed, asleep; the library book lying open where she had let it rest. Ella smiled, pulled a quilt over her and turned out the light. Then she went to bed herself.

As she fell asleep, she dreamt she was walking through a jungle. The air was unbearably humid, and she felt dwarfed by the scale of the verdant plant life. A huge drop of warm water fell from somewhere above, landing on her arm. The drop felt very realistic, she thought. She stood for a moment, disorientated. The green air was noisy, alive, buzzing. Insects? She could feel herself beginning to sweat, despite her lightweight dress. Very realistic, she thought once more: too realistic. I wonder if there is anybody about.

'Lucy?' she cried.

No answer.

'Luka?' she tried, half-heartedly.

No answer. Why would there be, she thought. Luka is in Quar, not in a jungle that's goodness knows where. There was nothing for it but to start walking.

She made her way along the path as best she could. It was a very rough track; sometimes it seemed to disappear altogether, but then she would pick it up again. She had no idea where she was, or where she was going, but she carried on regardless. She heard the roar of water long before she saw it. At first, she thought it was going to be a river, but then cliffs loomed up ahead, and a great waterfall could be seen cascading over moss-covered rocks. Finally, she fought her way out through the last of the vine-strangled tree trunks to stand by a lagoon. The waterfall fell down the centre of a horseshoe of cliffs, disappearing into a cloud of mist at its foot.

'You made it then!' said a familiar voice.

'Lucy!' she cried. 'You're here! But wait, where are we?'

'Good question. Either we're in my library book, or we are back where we wanted to be, only not exactly. From what I can remember of the map, we are absolutely nowhere near Quar; we're on the other side of the Kingdom.'

Lucy was waving her hand around, trying to demonstrate their location, and the ring caught Ella's eye. 'Is that the ring?' she asked, grabbing her sister's hand. 'I love the crown! Can I try it on?'

'No. I have to guard it with my life. That was the whole point of us leaving. At least, I think it was. Listen,

why don't you have some fruit, and then we're going into the waterfall,' she said, taking her sister quite by surprise.

'Whatever do you mean?' asked Ella.

'On the mosaic map on the wall in Quar, it showed the waterfall standing between the jungle and the plain. I think there might be a doorway. It's a good thing we spent so long getting ready in that bathroom!'

Lucy was sounding very confident, but if she was honest, she did not really think that there would be a way through the waterfall. Still, it was worth trying.

After Ella had eaten, they stepped into the water. They waded slowly, step by step, and found it pleasantly cool after the tropical heat. It began to get deeper until Ella had to swim, which was fairly tricky with shoes on. She held on to Lucy, and as they approached the cloud of spray, the noise was terrific.

'I don't think we can do it. We'll drown!' shouted Lucy above the din. She turned and helped drag her sister back to shallower waters. Climbing out, they threw off their waterlogged shoes and sat with their clothes sticking to their backs.

'So much for my hunch,' huffed Lucy.

'What was that?' asked Ella suddenly, pointing. 'I saw a rainbow.'

'It's probably the effect of the sun on the spray,' replied her sister despondently.

'No. *In* the water. A rainbow just jumped out! And there, another one.'

'Oh,' said Lucy. 'They're butterfly fish. They're really good in stews,' she added, remembering the meal she had once eaten on board *The Sienna*.

There seemed to be about half a dozen fish that were swimming about and jumping over the surface of the water. They were swimming really close to the girls.

'No wonder they're easy to catch,' said Lucy.

'But I think they're trying to get our attention! They're coming too near us for it to be normal, don't you think?'

'Maybe,' said Lucy thoughtfully. 'Put your shoes on, El, I've got a feeling you might be right.'

Quickly, the girls did up their soggy shoes and stood up. The fish appeared to respond to their movement and began to swim along the bank. Lucy followed, shoes squelching, as far as the edge of the cliffs. The fish sparkled on the surface, ripples spreading outwards.

'What are they waiting for?' asked Ella.

Suddenly, Lucy guessed it. There was a narrow ledge running along the edge of the horseshoe. It followed along the foot of the cliff, disappearing right behind the waterfall. She stepped cautiously onto it, her back pressed to the wall. Facing outwards, she began to shuffle sideways. The fish exploded out of the water in all directions, resembling some sort of firework, before beginning to swim towards the falls.

'I think that means we're on the right track!' she said excitedly. 'Come on. Just take it slow. Don't slip, whatever you do!'

Ella climbed on and began to shuffle sideways, copying her sister's movement. As they came near the foot of the waterfall, the air liquefied, and mist and spray rendered them temporally blind. Lucy could only hold her breath and inch forward. What was she thinking, following fish? All that she hoped was that Ella was safe.

Meanwhile, Ella was feeling the same about Lucy as they carried on as best they could.

They began to regain their sight and their ability to breathe just at the same time that they felt the ledge widen. They found themselves right behind the waterfall now, on a flat shelf. If they went far enough back into it, they could almost escape the spray.

'Now what?' shouted Ella, catching her breath.

'I don't know. Check the wall!'

They began to search the rocky surface for a door. It looked pretty hopeless, covered as it was in algae and slime, but then Ella found it. 'Here!' she shouted, excitedly. 'Pass me the stone!'

'What stone?' Lucy shouted back.

'The moon-shaped one that unlocks things!' she replied, as Lucy came close. Sure enough, Ella had found a little crescent-shaped hole in the surface.

'But I don't have it. Jethro does,' she said, her heart sinking. Her answer was almost inaudible. 'All he gave me was the ring and the letter,' she added, even more quietly. Or did he? She felt in her pocket and pulled out the letter. He had folded it before he gave it to her. She unfolded it carefully, trying to protect it from the elements. There, safe in the middle of the slender parcel, was the stone!

'How does he always manage to be one step ahead?' she wondered, relieved, as she posted it through the slimy hole. In an instant, the door revealed itself, and they pushed together until it slid into the rock face. They had entered a tunnel. It was not as dark as the cave they had last been in, and there was daylight up ahead. 'I mustn't forget J's useful stone!' she remarked, her voice echoing in the chamber.

She felt on the wall inside until she found where the stone lay. As she picked it up, the door closed behind them.

'Come on!' said Ella excitedly. 'Let's find out what's on the other side!'

They raced through the tunnel and ran carelessly out into the daylight – straight into two hulking, fierce-looking guards, dressed from head to toe in black. The peacock's feather and the eye served to confirm their plight.

The guards were taken quite by surprise, caught off guard, even, though not for long. 'Where did you two come from?' one of them snarled. His dark overgrown hair fell across cold, steely grey eyes.

Lucy thought fast, trying not to stare at the crumbs lodged in his unkempt moustache. He was a very untidy soldier. 'Oh, kind Sir,' she said, though he looked anything but kind. 'My sister and I are lost. We have been sleeping in that cave and just now we heard voices and thought you might be our father, here to find us!'

'You're miles from any town,' he said suspiciously. 'In truth, I think you're spies!'

'What are you accusing them of?' scoffed the other one, a fair-headed man with an equally mean look. 'Look at them; they're a couple of scrawny girls. What harm could they do to anyone?'

Lucy tried to make herself seem smaller and more frightened. Ella was petite, but right now she looked mad, like she was about to pick a fight, and Lucy threw her an urgent, cautionary look.

The men continued to argue, and Lucy thought they might almost be sent on their way, but then the dark-haired man won the argument. He went off to fetch some rope. The crisis pulled Lucy's thoughts into sharp focus.

'Please, can we just go and…' She made a face to suggest that they needed the toilet. He looked unmoved, until Ella pretended to cry. Disgruntled, he allowed them to go behind a shrub.

'Quick', whispered Lucy. 'Hide this in your underwear,' she said, handing Ella the letter. 'I think they'll be less likely to search you. Oh, and could you look a little more scared?'

'I am scared!' replied Ella meekly.

Lucy looked at her sister sympathetically. 'Me too,' she admitted, but she felt cool-headed as she put the stone into her shoe. Finally, with sudden inspiration, she used her hair bobble to put her hair into a bun, slipping the ring into its centre.

'Can you see it?' she whispered.

'No.'

'Good. Come on, then,' she said bravely. She took Ella's hand and reappeared from behind the bush.

The dark one had returned with rope and horses. He lifted Lucy and Ella roughly onto a handsome chestnut animal. Then he wrapped the rope around so that they were tied together, before lashing it to the horse's saddle. Wordlessly, their captors mounted up and set off with the girls' horse in tow.

I wonder where we are going, Lucy thought to herself miserably.

Chapter eighteen

Minutes turned to hours, and hours dragged by uncomfortably. Their shoes had finally dried out, but not before their feet had chilled. There was not a trace of tropical breeze here. Instead, over the endless plain blew a harsh wind that bit at their heels and pursued them tirelessly. As Lucy looked over the swaying grasses, she remembered the ride on her own horse, Bright Star. How different this was!

And she had so many questions. Where were they, and why were these soldiers so far from anywhere? Where were they going? How could they escape? Where were the others, and how could they find them? And she was thirsty, and hungry. Finally, when she could endure it no longer, she called out to the unspeaking foe. 'Please, kind Sirs, can we have some water to drink? I fear my sister won't last without it.'

The men grunted and shook their heads, muttering, as if it was a most unreasonable request, but then they began to slow up. When the three horses had come to a halt, the fair one jumped down and retrieved a flask from his saddlebag. He strode over to them and handed it up to Ella. At first she drank deeply, but then she began to cough, and Lucy felt her shudder. The man snatched the flask from her and thrust it into Lucy's hand. She was so thirsty, her tongue was stuck to the roof of her mouth, and she took a similarly deep draft of the liquid. It tasted bitter, and very quickly it began to burn her throat. She thought she might breathe fire, but instead she choked it down, grimacing. The eye on the man's uniform seemed to mock her as he took back the flask. 'That'll shut you up!' he snarled.

Lucy wondered what he meant, but then, as they set off again, she started to feel strange.

'Do you feel funny?' she whispered to Ella. Her sister was leaning heavily into her and gave no reply. Lucy felt increasingly drowsy, and the colours around her began to blur and merge. She could not focus her eyes. She squinted. This must be what it was like when someone took your glasses – she imagined, since she did not wear glasses. Then it hit her: they had been drugged! Frantically, she fought to stay awake, but it was no use. Sleep took hold of her.

Lucy would never find out how long they slept. But when she woke, she knew it must have been a very long time, because she was as hungry and thirsty as she could ever remember. Even more so, her head throbbed so much that she wished she could escape back to sleep. Ella lay next to her, still sleeping and looking as white as a sheet.

Lucy tried desperately to orientate herself. They seemed to be in some sort of prison cell. Mercifully, there was a jug of water and some bread and cheese left out on a table. She dragged her feet to the ground and walked gingerly over to it. She took only sips of water. It hurt to swallow, and her mouth stung painfully in protest, as if it had forgotten how to process food and drink. Slowly, the discomfort eased, and she risked a morsel of bread, dissolving it on her tongue. Now she tried a slightly larger piece, savouring the act of chewing. Just then, Ella began to stir, groaning.

Lucy poured a cup of water for her and shuffled back to the bed. She felt like an old lady, tired out by the effort of walking.

Ella sat up and rubbed her eyes. 'My head hurts!' she moaned, wincing at the pain.

'I know,' Lucy said sympathetically. 'It must be that flask they made us drink from. Here, have some water, slowly though!'

Ella sipped the water obediently and then handed the cup back. 'I might go back to sleep now,' she said weakly.

'No, El. I think we need to eat and drink and try to get our strength back. We need to exercise our legs. If you go back to sleep, you'll only get worse. Come on, I'll help you.'

Lucy helped her sister to sit up, and then moved her legs round. They sat side by side on the bed. Then she brought them each a hunk of bread and another glass of water. Slowly they worked on consuming the food, and little by little their headaches lessened and they began to feel less cold.

Lucy started to walk back and forth, stretching.

'Why are you limping?' asked Ella.

'Ah, that would be the stone in my shoe!' she replied.

'Of course!' laughed Ella, feebly. 'Where do you think we are?' she asked.

'I don't know. Look, there's a window up there, at the top of the wall. Maybe we could reach it?'

Lucy climbed onto the bed, and although she could touch the bottom edge of the window with her finger nails, she had no way to lever herself up so that she could see out.

'Perhaps you could go on my shoulders. I might be able to lift you, though I'm not feeling my strongest,' she admitted.

She sat down on the bed, and Ella climbed on. Then she stood and turned. After several attempts and much swaying and staggering, she managed to be standing on the bed with her sister above her. Ella held on to the bars of the window and looked out, her eyes at street level.

'We must be in a basement,' she said. I can see people going past. It's quite busy, lots of people. A town, perhaps? It smells... salty, I think?'

Just then, a face appeared in front of her. It was a little boy's. He stared at Ella, long and hard. 'Are you Lucy Butterfly?' he asked. 'I've seen a picture of you. My dad told me a story about you going on his ship.'

Before Ella could think of a reply to this most unexpected question, a great hand shoved the boy away from the window, and the boots of a soldier replaced the view. Ella wriggled in fright, and it took every ounce of energy Lucy had to stop them from falling backwards onto the floor. She managed to kneel and lower her sister safely. Now she could hear footsteps approaching, so she whispered urgently.

'Quick, lie down!'

They both lay quickly on the bed and tried to look as if nothing suspicious were happening. The door was unlocked and opened to reveal a man they had never seen before. He was wearing the enemy's uniform, but he was immaculately presented in comparison to the men who had brought them here. He had a bored, blank expression as he looked in their direction. 'You! Come with me!' he barked.

The girls began to move, to sit up.

'No. Not you!' he said flatly, addressing Ella. 'Just you, in the blue.'

Lucy felt her stomach knot, but perhaps it was for the best. 'Get some rest. I'll be back soon.' She patted her sister, smiling weakly. It was the best she could manage, before getting up from the bed and following after the guard. He continued to stare blankly, his eyes betraying not even a flicker of emotion. Lucy passed through the door, treading carefully so as to disguise her limp. She heard the key being turned in the lock behind her, but looked straight ahead, grateful that her sister was safe for now. The guard led the way along a narrow corridor and up a flight of steep stairs.

They were now in an entrance hall. There were two guards stationed in front of double doors. They stared forward. Beyond the doors, Lucy could see two more guards. They were standing back to back with the internal guards, and faced out on to the street. Four guards at the entrance – she wondered why there was such a high level of security.

Her escort knocked on a door to the right, and then proceeded to open it. He paused at the entrance, and Lucy understood that she should go in. The room she entered was panelled with a wood like mahogany. There was a window that faced on to the street and sunlight streamed in, falling on the surface of an enormous polished wooden desk. The floor was wooden too. On the wall opposite was the enemy's symbol, bold and defiant.

The man sitting at the desk gestured for Lucy to sit down in the chair opposite him. She sat, looking squarely at him, and shivered involuntarily. His hair was jet-black and oily, his skin so pale it looked almost grey. He had such dark circles under his eyes that he appeared as if he might be wearing bizarre makeup. Lucy wondered if the peacock's feather on the wall behind him had been positioned deliberately so as to give the illusion of a halo, or whatever the opposite of a halo might be. A ring of darkness perhaps, she mused, following her train of thought, trying to dwell on abstracts in an attempt to avoid the immediate.

'Would you like something to drink?' the man asked, his voice slick, almost snake-like.

There was a flask on the table, together with two cups.

'Are you going to drug me again?' asked Lucy bitterly.

'Heavens, no!' said the man smoothly. 'Some of my men are, shall we say, without scruples! I apologise. Here, I'll join you, to show you I mean you no harm.'

At this, he poured two glasses of a colourless liquid from the flask. He nudged one of the glasses in her direction, and then proceeded to take a drink from the other. Cautiously, Lucy took a sip of hers. It tasted like

elderflower, a little too sweet for her liking. She put the glass down.

'If you mean me no harm,' she levelled, 'why have you locked me in your dungeon? My sister and I were only lost. Now we are even more lost; I have no idea where I am, and my parents will be worried sick.'

'Really,' said the man. 'How touching. Well, first of all, you are in my town. That is where you are.'

He struck Lucy as incredibly arrogant. He was dressed differently to the other men she had seen. He was in black, true, but he had gold buttons on his uniform, and it was without the emblem. Clearly, he must be more important, in charge.

'In your town?' Lucy asked blankly. 'That's no help to me, Sir. I have no clue who you might be.'

She knew that she should be less brazen, but this man brought out the worst in her, and she felt a rising sense of outrage.

'What?! Have you been living under a rock? You seem strangely unafraid of your predicament.' He hesitated, seemingly unsure how to continue. 'Very well. I shall humour you, though I suspect you're playing some game with me. You are in the port of Salisman, and I am in control of this whole rotten Kingdom and all the trade that comes in and out. But now: enough. *I* will be asking the questions. Tell me, spy, why are you here, and who sent you?'

'As I told your men before, I'm no spy, nor is my sister. I'm here because I was dragged here, and what is more, nobody sent me. I'm only lost and in search of my family.'

'Really. But what were you doing so far out in the plains?'

'I told you. We got lost,' she sighed, frustratedly. 'We were travelling with my father, and then there was a storm and we became separated. We took shelter in a cave, and now we really need to find my father. You've dragged us miles and miles away, and now how is he going to find us?'

Lucy thought she sounded convincing. She tried to keep her expression open and honest. The man studied her quietly for some time, drumming his pale fingers on the desk until she began to feel quite unnerved. She took another sip of the sweet drink in order to steady her nerves.

'You see, I would like to believe you,' he began, 'but I think, in fact, that you were always planning to come here. We know that there are rebels gathering locally, but we don't know what they are planning. We have our suspicions, of course, but I would like you to tell me what you know.'

At least now he had put his cards on the table. But Lucy had no idea what he was talking about. She did wonder, though, if he might be right. Perhaps she was meant to come here after all.

'Rebels?' she asked, genuinely clueless.

'Yes!' he snapped. 'Rebels, from Quar. Tell me what you know!'

Lucy worked hard to keep her face blank. She tried to think of anything else so that she could stop thinking about Quar.

'Quar?' she said vaguely. 'But that is so far from here. I've never been to Quar,' she lied. 'My sister and I grew up in a small town in the mountains above the plain. This is the furthest we've ever been from home. Our parents will be so worried!'

At this point, she tried to look worried. It wasn't too difficult: his whole demeanour made her feel deeply unsettled. However, this was a game of bluffing. He knew very little, and how could he possibly know about her? Yet he was giving her invaluable information, and she hoped she might gain something more before the interview was over.

The man stood up and began to walk the floor. She used the opportunity to glance out of the window. The building opposite was a two-storey timber construction, and people were walking by, hurrying by, in fact. This was the enemy headquarters, and the guard presence was strong; it was not somewhere to loiter about. Then something caught her eye – a man and a small boy. They were walking slower than the others, and the boy was pointing. Then the man looked up, straight in the window, and his eyes fixed on Lucy. It was Captain Shaw! A flash of recognition, over in seconds, and the duo were gone. Lucy remembered the Captain transporting Jethro & herself to the Palace Isles on her first adventure. The boy must be his son, who had spoken to Ella through the window.

'What? What did you see?' thundered the man, interrupting her thoughts. He had been observing Lucy, and her face had given her away. How could she have been so foolish?

'Nothing,' she replied, too quickly. Then she added, 'Well, only, I saw a man who reminded me of someone I once knew, but it couldn't be, because he is back at home.'

'You are lying!' the man crowed, triumphantly. 'You will rot in my jail until I find out what I need to know. Think about that! Tomorrow, I shall try my luck with your younger sister. Perhaps she will do better at telling the truth!'

With that, he strode to the door and called for the guard. Lucy stood and walked out, shaken by the idea of Ella being grilled for information, but also buzzing with the thought that they might be in the right place after all.

Chapter nineteen

When she got back to the cell, Ella ran to greet her, hugging her in relief.

Lucy filled her in on everything that had happened, though she did it in whispers because she could not be sure that the guard was not hovering outside the door. She omitted to mention that the man was going to call Ella the next day – no need to worry her just yet.

They ate as much food as they could manage, and then retreated once more to the bed. It was frustrating being locked up, and now that they felt on the edge of something, they struggled to relax. The hints thrown out by the man had left them with questions and possibilities, and then there was the sighting of Captain Shaw. What could it all mean? It was not going to be easy to settle down, and Lucy took to pacing once more. At least her muscles were recovering. Ella preferred to lie down and watch.

The hours ticked by, and they knew it was night because it became dark inside, then out. In the end, Lucy gave up and settled down next to her dozing sister. She lay on her back listening to the quiet, but occasionally she could hear voices, horses' hooves and footsteps. It must have been getting late, but still she lay wide awake.

Suddenly she heard shouting, something about a fire! She could hear a commotion in the street – soldiers' boots and confusion. She sat up and walked over to the opposite wall, desperately trying to find some vantage point far enough away from the little window to be able to see out. It was no good.

'What is it?' asked Ella sleepily.

'Dunno. Nothing. Just some excitement going on outside. I can't see anything.'

Just then, there was a noise at their window. A boy's voice shouted down urgently. 'Move back, quick!'

Ella scrambled off the bed to join her sister, and seconds later they felt the room shake as dust and plaster started to fall from around the barred window. It gave a great creak, and then it was gone! Next, a rope fell down the wall, and the boy shouted once more. 'Climb up, quickly!'

Without a moment's thought, Ella raced up the rope with Lucy right behind her. In no time, they were out in the night air. It was thick with acrid smoke, and there were civilians and soldiers running about. The building across from the headquarters was ablaze, and every available person was passing buckets of water along in an attempt to quench the leaping flames. It looked like a pretty hopeless task. Lucy guessed it was all a distraction that Captain Shaw must have arranged to get them out.

'Come on!' said the boy. 'Follow me!'

He led them, running, down the cobbled street and round a corner, into a dark alley. Lucy ran for her life, so happy to be free. She ducked round the corner and straight into the arms of Jethro!

'J!' she cried. '*You're* behind this!'

'You didn't think I would return the favour?' he laughed. 'But this is no time for a reunion – let's get out of here! It won't take them long to realise you've gone.'

The little boy had paused next to Jethro, but now he was tugging urgently on his shirt.

'Oh, yes. Lucy, Ella, meet Enzo, Captain Shaw's son. Okay, I know, Enzo, we need to go. Take us to your dad!' he said.

'Hang on a minute!' Lucy pleaded. She leant down and removed the stone from her shoe. 'This is yours, I believe. It's making running very unpleasant!' She put the little stone in the palm of Jethro's hand.

Then they were off. Enzo was an expert at navigating the narrow streets of the port. He needed to be. Having memorised the soldiers' locations, he knew when they could afford to run and when they needed to sneak. There were no street lights, and the compact wooden houses leant in by their eaves to provide shade from the moon above. These were perfect shadowy conditions for making an escape. Nobody spoke as they travelled through the maze of streets that delivered them to the dock.

It was eerily quiet where the ships were moored. Everyone seemed to be asleep or out of sight indoors; it was safer not to break the curfew unless you really had to. Lucy could hear the familiar seaside sound of water lapping gently on the ships' hulls, and she noticed that the skyline to her right was comprised of varying heights of masts and sails jutting into the night sky. Just up ahead on the quay was a small contingent of soldiers, and as they crept nearer they could hear their muffled voices. They sounded rather animated, and the whole group was staring back in the direction of the town. The sky was glowing red from the fire, and Lucy only hoped that the blaze could be extinguished before it spread too far.

Between them and the soldiers was a generous pile of loaded sacks, and they ducked down behind, safely hidden from view for now. Enzo signalled to them, and they leant in close. He whispered as loudly as he dare. 'It's too dangerous tonight. We'll have to swim to Dad's ship. This way!'

As they watched, he retreated slowly and silently and then slipped into the murky water. One by one they followed, and Lucy could not help but gasp as the inky water wrapped its fingers around her. She began to worry about Jethro, but he must have learnt to swim after all, because he showed no signs of struggle. Once they were all in, Enzo began to swim along the length of the ship adjacent to them. They followed, keeping close together and feeling grateful that he was leading the way. When they reached the stern, they swam from craft to craft for what felt like forever, until he came to a stop next to a rope ladder.

'This is it,' he whispered. They were on the far side of a ship, safely facing away from the shore. He climbed nimbly up the ladder, followed by Ella, Lucy and lastly Jethro. Once over the edge, he led them below deck. It was pitch-black, but then he opened a hatch, and they found themselves in a room lit by candlelight.

'Welcome back to *The Sienna*, Lucy Butterfly!' said the friendly face of Captain Shaw. 'Enzo, you did a fantastic job!'

'So did you, Dad! How did you get back so quickly?'

'Well, I rode the horse hard until I was halfway, dragging that cell window of yours behind me. Then I untied the rope and left the thing lying in the street. I took the horse to the stable by the docks and then walked right up to the guards. They never suspect you if you act confidently enough, and they let me straight through! But now, let's get you all some blankets and get you dried out. Are you hungry? I'm sorry about us being down here, instead of in my cabins, but it's safer for us to stay out of sight. Let's get you some blankets. Zak!' he called out.

A door opened from the room beyond, and Zak appeared, with Luka right on his heels. Ella ran forward full of excitement, and still dripping. She greeted the twins while Lucy turned to Jethro, eyes wide with astonishment.

'And Mia?' she asked him.

'Yes, Mia too! We escaped. We're all safe. Even Nightfall has come along – she insisted, of course!' he answered, smiling.

'Mia's asleep,' the Captain chipped in, 'though I had a hard job convincing her. I promised you would look in on her when you got here, but I think it might be best to let her sleep. Morning will be soon enough.'

The blankets arrived, and every one huddled together in the room, too excited to go to sleep. Captain Shaw excused himself, but one of his men brought in a tray of hot drinks. It tasted like liquid melted marshmallows, and it warmed the children right down to their toes. Lucy wondered if she was being drugged all over again as a delicious drowsiness crept upon her.

Ella was now in her element, and thrilled to see Luka. She told him all about the jungle and the waterfall and their rescue. Enzo was listening in while playing a game of dice with Zak. It was a happy scene, and Lucy leant back against the wall, knees tucked up, arms clasped around them. She felt content, though if she cared to admit it, exhausted. Eyes closed, she listened to the chatter. The individual words blended into a soft cadence that seemed to recede into her subconscious as tiredness blurred her mind.

Just then, she felt someone sit down beside her. 'I missed you, Lucy,' Jethro said, his shoulder touching hers.

Lucy's eyes were still closed. 'Oh J, I missed you too,' she replied.

She leant her head against his shoulder. The last drops of adrenalin had all been used up, and the sum of all that jungle and waterfall, capture and escape, fear and joy, finally caught up with her.

When she woke, she was still leaning into him. In the stillness she could hear the slow, steady beat of his heart and feel the gentle rise and fall of his chest. He must be asleep. She opened half an eye and peered about, taking care not to move. Everyone appeared to be asleep, scattered across the floor under blankets, and Ella was just a few feet away. The candle was burning low. It must still be night, she thought, and went back to sleep.

When next she woke, Mia was sitting cross-legged on the floor, watching her. The little girl grinned, causing Lucy to start. Her movement disturbed Jethro, and he too woke. Mia smiled broadly at both of them as they straightened up and stretched themselves.

'Morning, Mia,' Jethro said in a low voice.

'Morning,' she said, climbing into his lap. She turned to Lucy. 'And I'm so glad to see you. Jethro was ever so worried about you.'

'Was he?' she answered softly. 'Well, I was worried about all of you as well. In fact, I've got something for you,' she continued.

Lucy tugged at her hair bobble until it began to slide. Her hair tumbled out over her shoulders, and the small gold ring clattered onto the floor. She picked it up. 'Try this for size, Mia,' she said. Taking hold of the girl's right hand, she slid the ring on to the ring finger.

'It fits just right!' exclaimed the little girl, admiring it. 'Is it really for me?'

Sure enough, when Lucy checked, she found that it did fit the princess's hand perfectly.

'Yes, I believe it's for you,' Lucy concluded happily. 'What time is it, Mia?' she asked, suddenly.

'Oh yes, I was supposed to tell you. It's breakfast time!'

'Okay, well run along, and tell the Captain that we'll get everyone up and ready. We'll be along shortly.'

Mia climbed out of Jethro's lap and skipped in and out of the sleeping bodies, off to fulfil her next mission. Silence descended once more.

'Does she know yet? You know, who she is?' Lucy asked.

'No. Not yet. We'll tell her when we need to.'

'Hey, I think the ship's moving. What do you think?'

'Hmm?' he replied distractedly.

'I said, I think the ship's moving. J, are you listening to me?'

'What? Oh yes, I think you're right. But Lucy, we need to talk. I have some things to tell you.'

He sounded a bit awkward, but Lucy did not stop to wonder why, for she too had news.

'Me too! I think Ella might have helped me solve the riddle, but let's find out where we're going first – and we better get this lot up for breakfast!'

'You're right. We can talk later,' he agreed, still pensive.

Chapter twenty

Everyone was in agreement. Fried fish was definitely the best breakfast there was, especially when eaten on the deck of *The Sienna*, as it cut its way through crystal waves, under a brilliant blue sky. It was difficult to imagine wars or prison cells – or any kind of sadness for that matter. Everything seemed perfect. Only the vigilant watchman in the crow's nest hinted at another reality. Captain Shaw explained that the seas were patrolled, but he had a permit to sail. THEY took from his profits, or even stole his cargo, according to their whim, calling it tax, but otherwise he continued his work as a sea trader.

After they had eaten their fill, Enzo was raring to show them around the ship, and most especially to show them the drawing his father had done of Lucy. Jethro excused himself, encouraging the others to go off and have fun, with the proviso that he keep Lucy.

'Come on, let's find an out-of-the-way spot,' he suggested to her.

They headed up towards the bow and found a sunny location. Sitting side by side with their backs to the railing, Jethro pulled out his notebook and began flicking through the pages, but then he let it drop and stared down at the deck, utterly miserable.

'What is it, J?' asked Lucy, 'I know it's something.'

Jethro lifted his eyes and turned to look at her. 'It's the King. News reached us before we left Quar. THEY executed him.'

There was a terrible silence, and Lucy felt her heart break. He had been a good and wise man, and her memory of him, though distant, was both fond and awed. But to Jethro, he had been something like a father and a guide. Poor Jethro, was all she could think. Time seemed to pause, but then it began to turn again slowly, and Lucy heard her mouth speaking. 'What?! No, that's awful. I'm so sorry; I wish I could have been there when you heard…'

'Anyway,' he continued with conviction, 'I won't let him down. I'll finish what he started. It's only served to strengthen my resolve.' He drew himself up and exhaled, seeming to file the painful truth somewhere in a recess of his mind.

If he could do it, she would too, Lucy thought.

Taking up the notebook once more, he continued. 'I've had a lot of time to read my notes. We spent several nights behind the painting before it was finally safe to get going. All the while, I was thinking about the Duke's revelation and the significance of Mia and how we might complete the square.'

'Yes,' agreed Lucy. 'I've been doing the same. Ella came up with this idea that you and Mia, Luka and Zak make up the four sides of the square, and that Ella and I have to get you into the right places.' She paused, hesitating. 'When she told me, it made perfect sense, but now that I repeat it to you, it sounds rather silly. How could you four holding hands in a square make any difference?' she concluded, doubtfully.

They were both quiet for a moment, but then Lucy tried again. 'The thing is, I found out about completing the square.' Her mind flashed back to the laptop in the café. 'It's mathematics. Arrange things in the correct form and the easy solution presents itself, something like that. I really thought I saw the solution. It felt right, and I couldn't wait to tell you. But now...' her voice trailed off uncertainly.

Jethro was looking through his book. 'You know, I had a similar experience. You get a glimpse. It's like standing in the pitch-black, then for one second there's light, and you see all these images and ideas, and then just as quickly, it's dark again. If you don't trust what you saw, it'll be lost. You'll convince yourself that you made it up, that it's all nonsense.'

'Yes, that's right! Did you see something then?' asked Lucy, suddenly encouraged.

'Yes, clear as day, I saw Mia on a throne, but the throne was an ancient ruin. It was so vivid, I even sketched the throne room.'

'And?'

'And, I've read about a ruin, where our kings used to be crowned long ago, at the foundation of the Kingdom.'

'So, what are we waiting for, let's go there!' said Lucy.

'We're already on our way. Captain Shaw is taking us up the coast as we speak,' Jethro replied modestly.

'Oh, J! How did you get so smart!' she groaned. 'I'm really not sure what you need me here for!' She was joking, but there was still a question in there somewhere, and he heard it.

'I need you because you're brave and brilliant, because you bring out the best in me. It's like we belong, Lucy. I need you because…'

She did not let him finish. 'I know,' she said softly. 'You're my closest friend in the entire world. You know me.'

They fell comfortably silent, yet awkward at the same time. Somehow they had managed to communicate how they felt.

'I should go and check on the others,' Lucy said at length.

'Okay,' he agreed, but he still looked troubled.

Lucy wondered if he was thinking about his friend the King again, and she took his hand in hers, hoping in some way to comfort him.

'I think we could be facing danger,' he confessed solemnly.

'That's why you've got me,' she said cheerfully. 'Brave and brilliant, remember?!'

'True!' he said, managing a smile, before she left him.

As they were nearing their destination, the Captain gathered them together in his cabin to explain what must happen next. 'Listen up, everyone. We're entering dangerous seas now. This is an area that seems to be of special interest to our enemy, so I'm afraid there's a real risk of being boarded. I'll do my best to get us to an unguarded spot, and hopefully we can get you ashore without detection. However, in the meantime, I need you all hidden away until I give the all clear. Do you understand?'

A chorus of 'Yes, Sirs' confirmed to him that they did, and Enzo led them down into the bowels of the vessel, to a small room full of wooden barrels.

'You can sit behind those barrels,' he suggested. 'If we have any trouble, I'll try as best I can to get you a signal, and maybe you could climb inside to hide. Okay?'

'Okay, Enzo, thanks!' said Jethro.

'First we're flour sacks and now we get to be barrels of …' Ella sniffed in one of the empty barrels '… fish!' she confirmed, grimacing.

'Let's hope it doesn't come to that, El,' said Lucy.

They settled themselves at the back of the room, well shielded from view, behind the barrels. It was an effective, though not very pleasant, hiding place, being dark and airless, and only Nightfall was happy about the smell.

'I wonder how long we'll be stuck here,' Zak complained impatiently.

'I'm sure time will fly,' responded Luka, always able to see the bright side. 'Lucy could tell us a story.'

The stories ran out long before the wait ended, and after a while there was nothing but the movement of the sea to entertain them. Lucy pictured the swell as the ship rose and fell, high then low. The highs felt like they were reaching ever higher, the lows plunging steadily lower. The weather must have changed; perhaps there was a storm coming? The motion was hypnotic, comforting, as if they were being held high in the arms of some benevolent giant who was gently rocking them to and fro. Her meditations built courage within her because, despite being on the brink of unknown danger, she understood that she was being held. She felt secure, inexplicably peaceful.

Enzo broke the spell when he stumbled into the room. 'Hey, how's it going, everyone? The weather's coming in!' he confirmed. 'We're passing enemy ships, small crafts, all sorts. It's really tricky sailing, but so far no one has asked to board. I've never seen so much activity! I'm afraid you're going to be down here a bit longer, but I brought you some food. Now I'd better get back up top.'

With that he disappeared, leaving behind a tray balanced on one of the barrels. There was a candle on it, so they could see their meal and the walls of their hiding place.

'Let's stand up and stretch our legs,' suggested Jethro. 'Anyone hungry?' he asked, beginning to cut the bread and hand it out with hunks of cheese. A bowl of dried berries disappeared in minutes, washed down with fizz from a flask. The meal was quickly done with, and they took their places once more behind the collection of barrels. They continued to wait.

'Tell us about this ruin we're going to, J?' asked Lucy at length.

'I don't know much,' he admitted. 'I just know where we have to start our search. Have you heard of Peridan Lighthouse?'

'I have!' said Zak. 'It's the oldest lighthouse in the Kingdom, and the biggest and the grandest. But the light doesn't work any more, does it?'

'That's right. It was one of the first things THEY took over when they invaded, and no sooner had they done so than they put out the light. And their ships patrol the area endlessly, so that it's almost impossible to reach.'

'But what has that got to do with our ruins?' asked Lucy.

'Well, in all my research I've never been able to find any ruins on a map, and yet I've found them referred to as the ruins of Peridan. So I can only assume that our destination is somewhere in that vicinity. But the lighthouse is guarded, as is the sea that surrounds it, so…'

'So we'll need to have our wits about us!' interpreted Zak.

'Yes, exactly,' agreed Jethro. 'It might be tricky, but we've already broken into cities and out of jails, so I think that together we'll find a way to do this.'

His words sounded confident, but his eyes betrayed him. Lucy watched her friend in the candlelight. She was proud of the way he led them, proud of who he had become, and she knew what she wanted to say.

'Yes, Jethro's right,' she said. 'We will find a way to do this. Do you know what? It might sound funny to say this, but we're not on our own. The sea is our friend. I felt it just now, like I was being held in its arms.'

Suddenly, her thoughts were unlocked and the ideas flowed freely. 'The more I think about it,' she continued passionately, 'the more strongly I'm persuaded the whole Kingdom is our friend – it wills us to succeed! It cheers us on, longing for the enemy to be banished from its borders. If the land could cry out, it would. In fact, that's what "the miracle of the desert" is about, don't you see? The

Kingdom's getting ready for things to be set right. That's why we have to complete the square!'

Jethro was smiling now – everyone was. Lucy made sense because she had observed something true. Not the kind of truth that you could see or touch, but the kind of truth that you could not deny. Deep down, you knew it was true.

'I'm ready to go to the lighthouse now!' said Mia eagerly. Her cat mewed in agreement, and everyone else laughed lightly.

They had only recently fallen silent when the door burst open. It was Enzo. 'THEY are on board! Dad told me to hide with you! Quickly, blow the candle out, hide the tray!'

Seconds later, they were squatting in the darkness. They had decided to take their chances where they were; the barrels were just too unappealing.

Enzo breathed heavily, trying to catch his breath, and he trembled slightly. Lucy put a hand on him. 'Your dad will be safe, Enzo. You mustn't worry,' she whispered.

Now they could hear shouting and banging. The ship was being searched inch by inch, and it sounded like things were being torn apart, smashed and kicked over. What would happen if the barrels were pushed around? The children shrank deeper into the shadows as the noises came closer.

The hide and seek came to a terrifying head as the door crashed open, and two burly men stood as silhouettes framed by the doorway. 'What's this stinking room then?' asked one, disdainfully.

'Rotten fish! You search it!' the other grunted.

'No, you!' said the first, childishly.

One of the reluctant soldiers walked towards the barrels and half-heartedly lifted the lids off a couple. His inspection drew to a halt.

'Nothing in there. Besides, a spy would probably die in one of these. They're disgusting!'

As he turned to go, Luka relaxed slightly and shifted his weight, unwittingly knocking the tray near his foot. The flask fell with a clatter. It was a horrible moment that he would not forget for a long time to come.

The man spun back round, and his partner came up beside him. 'Did you hear that?' he cried. 'I think we should take a better look, don't you?'

Suddenly, brilliantly, Nightfall sprang onto the barrel in front of the two guards. He miaowed sweetly and licked his paw. What an actor!

'Aw, it's only the ship's cat!' said the soldier. 'Been having yourself a meal, I expect?' he said, stroking the cat.

Nightfall jumped down from the barrel, sauntered through one of the men's legs, rubbing against it and purring loudly before heading for the open door. He turned to make sure that the men had taken the bait and then continued on. The soldiers gladly followed him out, keen to end their search of the more dismal parts of the ship.

'That was too close,' breathed Lucy, when she was sure they had gone, and no one sought to contradict her.

'I hope we get there soon,' longed Ella.

'Now wouldn't be soon enough,' agreed Zak drily.

Chapter twenty-one

The storm blew through, and a stillness fell upon the waters, leaving a thick fog clinging to the coastline, as the Captain and his men approached the lighthouse at Peridan. The white building rose proudly out of the low cloud, standing tall on the clifftop. They were still navigating their way past enemy craft, and the Captain wondered how on earth he would find a safe place to dispatch his precious cargo. There was nothing for it but to carry on.

Leaving the lighthouse behind them, Shaw found what he was looking for – a deserted cove. The last sighting of an enemy craft had been half an hour earlier. It was one of those blackened patrollers, with the sail that looked like the leathery skin of a bat's wing. The Captain could never understand why they chose to make their fleet look as if it had barely escaped the flames of some great battle.

But no matter, the vessel had waved him on, and he had headed to the secluded spot. The ship neared the coast cautiously, feeling its way as though one blind. Indeed, the fog was at its thickest here, and he could risk going no further, so he put down the anchor. A small rowing boat disappeared into the cloud, containing two of his men he had sent out to check the lie of the land. The Captain waited nervously for news, but they returned shortly and reported the all-clear. He went below deck to bring Jethro the news.

'Jethro, Lucy, children!' he called, as he swung the door open. 'We're here, it's time!'

The children gladly followed him out of their confinement and back onto the deck. They were greeted by the warm, damp air and everything looking blurry and white.

'Where are we?' asked Jethro, trying to get his bearings.

'About a mile and a half south of the lighthouse, as the crow flies, at least. Might be more like two or two and a half, if you're walking. You'll need to pick your way along the cliffs. At least the weather is on your side; it'll give you some cover,' the Captain concluded.

'Thanks, Captain, for risking your crew and even your son Enzo, for our sake. We can't thank you enough,' Jethro said.

'Not at all,' he replied humbly. 'What you're doing, you're doing for all of us. I've seen what you and Lucy can accomplish once already, and I'd give anything to see you win this one – and you will, I feel it, just like I felt it the last time. I'm daring to hope, and I don't expect to be disappointed.'

'Thanks,' said Jethro, feeling buoyed up by the heartfelt encouragement.

'Yes, thanks!' said Lucy, hesitating over a handshake, then opting instead for a hug.

'Godspeed!' he wished them. 'Now, hurry. Be on your way, and remember – be careful!'

The children climbed down into the waiting rowing boat. Nightfall perched on Mia's lap, his tail flicking, his eyes ranging to and fro in the white air. They all stared out into the fog as the boat made its way back to the shore. It was a comfort to be so completely hidden from sight, yet they could not help thinking that the enemy would have exactly the same advantage. Accordingly, it was with trepidation and great stealth that they climbed from the boat, silently waving their goodbye to the crewman.

The cove was narrow and the beach almost an afterthought of the sea. At its perimeter, Jethro found a trail and motioned for the others to follow. It was in single file that they began to ascend, as it wound very gradually upward before levelling out. The pathway ran like a scar along the cliff side of rock, rough grasses and bracken. At intervals, clumps of hardy flowers had dug their roots down stubbornly; they must have had a taste for the salty air.

As time passed, the sense of isolation slowly eased their apprehension, and they began to enjoy themselves a little. The mist was thinner at this middle height on the cliff, and the soft light enabled Zak to take over the lead as lookout and scout. He was unconcerned for a long while, but the lighthouse was now looming close, and they would soon round the last curve in the cliff side. Below them in the sea would be the army of vessels that the Captain had warned them about. The children were still somewhat cloaked by the cloud, but there was a breeze blowing, and visibility was undeniably improving.

'Wait here,' Zak suggested at this point. 'Why don't you eat something, and I'll take a look beyond the headland.'

Everyone was glad for a rest as Zak went off on his own. At least, he thought he did.

As he rounded the bend, he observed that the rocky cliff face was pocked with holes. The wind had etched a network of recesses, and even now he heard it whispering and working away at the surface. Here and there, white seabirds had made their nests, and they sat silently, in ones and twos, bracing themselves on this windy spot. The path up ahead looked clear but he could see the shadowy ships in the water below.

He turned to go back with his report and nearly jumped out of his skin. Nightfall was on the path, and from his posture Zak was left in no doubt of the cat's intentions. Belly to the ground, he was inching forward in slow motion, eyes gleaming.

'Nightfall! No!' hissed Zak, but it was too late. The cat sprang onto the hillside, jumping for the bird nearest to his position. A perfect surprise, he clipped its wing before it rose into the air, squawking a terrible cry of alarm. To Zak's horror, the cat jumped from nest to nest, and a whole crowd of crazed seabirds flapped and cried, flying in all directions. What was probably about a hundred birds seemed to become a thousand, and the cat might as well have set off a flare and announced to the enemy that they had arrived. Zak threw himself to the ground and lay flattened and powerless as the deafening clamour exploded all around him. When finally it subsided, he peered over the edge. Taller than all the other vessels, a solitary mast poked through the wispy, thinner fog, and Zak was sure he could make out the circular glass of a telescope from a crow's nest.

He lay back down, breathing heavily. Perhaps they had seen the birds and thought nothing was untoward. It was a possibility. Just then, Nightfall came to inspect him lying on the path. He rubbed himself against Zak's arm and then nosed his hand.

'Hello, kitty cat,' whispered Zak miserably. 'I know, you couldn't help it!' he sighed, 'All those tasty birds.'

In the end, he decided there was nothing for it but to retreat by wriggling on his stomach until he was beyond the bend. Once he had made it, he jogged back to the others.

'What on earth happened?' cried Lucy as he arrived.

'Nightfall happened – to some seabirds! I think I might have been spotted,' he added glumly.

'Right, well, that confirms it then,' said Jethro. 'We need to abandon this path and climb up top. Let's come at this from a different side. Then, if they're watching the cliffs, we might still slip in unawares.'

Lucy tried to assess the climb – there were lots more rocks and plants. It was steep, but not impossibly so, and Ella and Luka were already eagerly tackling the first section. Mia was thinking about scolding her cat, but instead she gave him a tickle under his chin. He was too dear to shout at. Meanwhile, Zak had his share of the food, and then they followed together, scrambling upwards, with Jethro bringing up the rear.

They reached the clifftop without incident. The mist had dispersed completely at the top, and they stood in a knot, fully visible and feeling vulnerable.

'We can't stay here. We're hopelessly exposed!' said Lucy, stating the obvious.

'She's right,' agreed Zak. 'What do we do, Jethro?'

'Well, we need to get a look in the lighthouse. It's the only clue we have. We could wait until dark, or perhaps it's safe. The place seems deserted.'

'I could check it out, but only on one condition,' Zak added.

'Go on?' asked Jethro.

'You keep hold of the cat this time!'

'Deal! We'll duck down here at the edge and wait.'

It was an unpleasant kind of waiting. It all felt very wrong. It was too quiet, too deserted. They had expected the area to be guarded. Why guard the sea and not the lighthouse itself? Lucy felt herself shivering, yet it was not cold, and she wondered if she was becoming ill. Her skin felt cold and feverish, and the hair on the back of her neck stood on end. A cold feeling of dread and foreboding was settling on all of them. Jethro saw her trembling and put his arm strongly round her.

'I feel it too,' he told her. 'Zak will come back with bad news, if he comes back at all.'

She leant into him, trying to find some warmth and comfort, but the oppression only increased. Just then, Zak returned. He looked unseasonably cheerful, and his news baffled them.

'All clear! There's no one about, and the place seems abandoned. The enemy was here, but not any more.'

'Are you sure, Zak? It feels so cold, like the enemy is right upon us,' Lucy observed.

'Really? I saw no one,' Zak replied unequivocally.

'What do you think, J?' she persevered. 'The enemy's here, don't you agree?'

'I do,' he said slowly. 'Something's not right, but what choice do we have?'

Jethro could feel the darkness, the absence of hope, just as clearly as Lucy, but they could not afford to stop now. They had to face the unknown head on; it was a necessary risk.

'Everyone, listen,' he said, finally making up his mind. 'We're going into the lighthouse, there's nothing for it. We'll stick together and we'll be okay. Godspeed!'

'Godspeed!' everyone murmured in unison.

There was some relief to be had in the simple fact that the waiting was over. Jethro stowed his bag under a shrub, and then they rose together and walked the last half mile out in the open. Lucy tried to overcome her sense of dread by making her gait confident and her posture defiant, but she felt like a lowly grasshopper advancing on a lion. In her mind, the lighthouse was poised to pounce. Yet she shrugged off the image and told herself repeatedly that the whole Kingdom stood behind them, willing them to win. She gripped Mia's hand as well as Ella's and felt the solidarity of all her comrades as they advanced on towards their destination.

The lighthouse was a ghostly white and held itself like some monument to a past age. Without its light, it was devoid of value: an empty mausoleum. Lucy felt that it seemed to be working by some perverse method contrary

to its nature, drawing them onto the rocks to crash, rather than warning them to stay away. She tried to shake off these morose images. The worry and fear was doing its best to intimidate her.

At last they stood at the foot of the towering, cylindrical edifice. The entrance was by a single door, with one way in and one way out. Jethro turned the handle and stepped resolutely inside, followed by everyone else, until Lucy closed the door behind them. They had made it inside, and none of the scenarios she had envisaged had come to pass: no lion had eaten her, no grave had swallowed her, and she did not lie shipwrecked. Perhaps she was imagining all this drama!

Instinctively, they began to climb up to the top, up to see the lamp. The steps were spiral and, despite their steady conviction, they stopped on each level to look in the rooms. Each one was circular and simply whitewashed, but the rooms hinted at grandeur nevertheless. There was a kitchen on the first floor, a comfortable living room on the second and a bedroom on the third. The rugs on the floors and all the fabrics were ornate, yet faded and dusty, smelling of absence and loss.

The higher they climbed, the more reckless they felt, as if the altitude were making them giddy. If this was a trap then they were walking right into it. In spite of this, they all felt a momentary relief from their stealth and concealment. Ella chatted excitedly, telling Zak and Luka about a lighthouse she had visited once with her grandfather. They had gone in the boat at night and watched the light blinking like a great eye.

Jethro had to help Mia up the last few stone steps, and finally they arrived, all six of them and a cat, together at the very top. The room was open and bright with a view out across the sea. The enemy vessels appeared like imprecise pencil sketches drawn upon swatches of misty white and blue. The lamp had been smashed to pieces, and they stood together around its remains.

'What was its power source?' Lucy asked, wondering how a lighthouse operated without electricity.

'I don't know,' Jethro replied. 'I wasn't sure this place was more than a myth. I don't know anything about it really.'

He took his notebook out and flipped randomly through the pages. 'There was nothing about this place in here; it was only the vision I had. Remember?'

'Yes. The ruins at Peridan, I remember,' Lucy said.

Zak went to look again at the ships under the mist. They appeared to be gathering like a swarm of bees far below, and he felt sick in the pit of his stomach. It was nothing the others had not felt earlier, and now he began to understand their discernment. Jethro went to join him.

'I don't like the look of that. What now?' Zak commented.

'Honestly, Zak, I don't know.'

Just then, Lucy called over. She was standing beside Mia at the back of the room.

'J, you'd better come and see this!'

There was a simple name plaque on the wall that had been carved out of stone. It had the word 'Peridan' in its centre, and around its border were stars. In the left corner was a hole in the shape of a crescent moon.

Jethro pulled the little stone key out of his pocket and posted it into the hole, but on this occasion nothing happened. The stone simply vanished, unlocking nothing. Before there was time for disbelief or any other response, they heard a noise: footsteps.

It was not just one set of footsteps, but many: the steady rhythm of heavy soldiers' boots on the stone stairs. It was an especially chilling sound because there was no escape, and they knew it. All they could do was wait together and meet their fate.

Chapter twenty-two

The first soldier to reach them was the man who had held Lucy and Ella in his jail. Behind him spilled in half a dozen of his men. He was panting from the exertion and his usually grey face was slightly tinged with colour; Lucy surmised he probably spent a lot of time behind his desk. His troops, clearly fitter, were quite composed as they stared blankly at their prey. There was such a cold, lifelessness in their eyes that even the eye on their uniform seemed more compassionate.

'Well, well, what have we here?' their jailor gloated when he had finally caught his breath. He looked crow-like, or perhaps vulture-like; certainly cruel and mocking. 'The runaway rebel and her gang! I just knew you were at the heart of this plot. Your "lost girl from the mountains" act didn't fool me for a second!'

Lucy stepped towards him, feeling strangely bold. The smashed parts of the lamp were the only obstacle separating them. 'You've got me,' she said, putting her hands in the air. 'I'm the mastermind. Getting caught at the top of an empty lighthouse – pretty brilliant, eh?'

She had nothing to lose and everything to gain. Her proud jailor had given her information before; perhaps he would oblige once more. The man studied her suspiciously, but then he seemed to relax, confident in having the upper hand. If he had been walking about, it would surely have been with a strut.

'Oh, I like you! Always playing the innocent girl so well. As if you don't know the significance of this place. We both know that if you'd found a way to relight this thing, it would've been the end for us – our right to remain would've been revoked, so to speak. But of course you have not; we damaged it beyond repair, and you've walked neatly into my trap. So predictable – though what else should we expect from mere children!'

'Well, you have me now, and you've won. So why don't you let the others go? You can do what you want with me,' Lucy bargained.

'Oh no,' said the man darkly. 'There'll be no more jailbreaks for you or your friends; not even the cat will escape this time.'

He turned to the soldier nearest to him and issued an order. 'You! Take the animal and escort the prisoners to the ground floor. I want their hands tied, and I want them locked in the store cupboard. We'll wait for the other patrols to arrive before we move out.'

With that, the man turned on his heels, and his men parted so that he could leave. The soldiers then began to close in around the children. One of them reached down to pick up Nightfall, who arched his back, hissing, and before the man could retract his hand, the cat had gashed his sharp claws across it. Pained, the unfortunate soldier nursed it, cursing quietly.

At this point, Mia stepped in. 'I'll carry him,' she said airily, 'unless you want to experience him *really* angry!'

The man grunted his consent, and the little girl whisked up her pet and cradled him in her arms, trying to soothe his temper. The children were now escorted back down the stairs. Like Lucy's, Jethro's pulse was racing. However, it was more from excitement than from fear because now they knew what they needed to do. They had to reilluminate the light.

When they arrived back on the ground floor, the guards began to tie their hands behind their backs. Lucy had to protest. 'This girl is five years old. Look at her! She couldn't hurt a fly. Surely you don't have to tie her up.'

The guard looked at Mia. She was small and frail-looking, and her green eyes seemed to hypnotically whisper to him, 'Trust me'. So he went against orders and left the girl free. Once everyone else had been bound, they were herded roughly into the storeroom opposite the door. A soldier ordered them to sit and, once satisfied, closed the door and turned the key. They heard him ordering four of his men to stand guard, and then it became less noisy. A small window high up on the wall behind them shed a sliver of light, so that at least they could see each other.

'Quick, Mia! Untie us,' whispered Jethro.

Mia tried her best, but the ropes had been expertly tied, and she could not loosen even one of the bindings. Having tried each one in turn, she slumped back onto the floor, disheartened.

'You were right, Lucy,' she whispered, crestfallen. 'They didn't need to tie me up; I'm no danger and no use.'

'Oh Mia, don't worry, the knots are too tight. We'll think of something else, but thanks for trying!'

For a time they sat together in silence. Occasionally there was a commotion outside the door as a new patrol arrived and checked in. They dreaded to think what a vast number of soldiers were gathering. Nightfall was pacing back and forth like a tiger in a cage. Every now and then he would utter a yowl of discontent that perfectly captured the mood. It was a mixture of frustration and fright. Then he would begin his pacing again.

'Please stop it,' said Mia finally. 'Come and sit!' she begged.

The cat desisted and made as if to walk towards his mistress, but then he paused next to a portion of the wall. He began to paw the ground, mewing, and then picked something up in his mouth. Mia wondered at his strange behaviour, but after all, her cat was often doing something unpredictable. Nightfall sauntered back to his mistress and dropped his find on the ground in front of her.

'What it is?' she asked, stroking him between his ears, but then she snatched up the object and jumped up rather dramatically. Everyone had been daydreaming, trying to think of things other than their predicament, but they soon took notice when she waved her arms about.

'Look what Nightfall found!' she whispered as loudly as she dare. She was holding the stone, the crescent moon-shaped stone!

'It must have travelled down through the wall!' gasped Jethro softly. 'Quick, start looking everyone! There must be another keyhole somewhere in this room!'

Everyone struggled quietly to their feet and spread out around the room. They began to search inch by inch, becoming increasingly frantic, because the level of activity outside the door was beginning to increase. Corporately, they willed there to be a keyhole, and finally they found it. The cat discovered it. It was in a skirting board that ran at floor level, and Mia had found him pawing at it. He was certainly a bright creature. Everyone held their breath and waited full of suspense as Mia posted the stone into the moon shape. A panel in the floor began to shift, sliding downwards until it was swallowed into the darkness. There was now a compact, black square in the floor. Nightfall shot down into the hole and disappeared.

As the only one with her hands free, Mia volunteered to go first. She slid in and disappeared, and seconds later her head reappeared. 'There are steps leading down. I can see a light at the end. Once you're inside, you'll see it. Come on!'

One by one, they entered the hatch feet first, feeling for the promised steps beneath them. It was awkward without arms and hands for balance, but everyone was steady by determination. Mia waited patiently until they were all inside.

'We need to close it behind us,' Jethro whispered to her. 'Can you help me? Can you find the key?'

Mia felt on the wall by the entrance, and sure enough the key was on a shelf. As she lifted it, the trapdoor began to close behind them. Jethro ducked out of the way with Mia holding on to him. It was suddenly very dark, but sure enough, there was a small rectangle of light further down. Jethro leant his shoulder against the wall for balance and began the climb down. He could hear the others doing the same ahead of him and saw their shadows pass into the light.

As he caught up with them, he found himself in a spacious and bright, airy cavern. Lucy ran up to him, all smiles and relief. She would have thrown her arms around him, but it was physically impossible! Suddenly, everyone was talking at once.

'We're safe, J, we did it!' marvelled Lucy.

'This is it! This is the place I saw: the ruins of Peridan!' exclaimed Jethro in amazement.

'Can you imagine the look on their faces!' laughed Zak to himself.

'Good pussy cat! Clever pussy cat! Fresh fish for you, very soon, I promise!' cooed Mia over her cat.

'Look, Luka, I can see the sea. We must be in the cliff face under the lighthouse,' calculated Ella.

'Now we just need to escape these ropes,' noted Luka quietly.

Everything they said was true, and perhaps they should have taken turns and listened to each other, but adrenalin coursed through each of them, and they could not help themselves. However, slowly they calmed down and came together again.

The cavern was an unusual blend of natural and man-made architecture, as if pieces of a palace had been transplanted into this bizarre location. For though the ceiling and the walls were the exposed rock of a cave, much of the floor was covered with geometric-patterned tiles that were black and white, terracotta and turquoise. Granted, the tiles had worn down to bare rock in many places, yet they could imagine its previous grandeur.

They found six stumps of rock protruding from the floor, and Luka guessed correctly that they had once been pillars. On the walls were wooden cupboards overlaid with silver leaf that had been carved with a forest of trees. The silver, though badly tarnished, had preserved the wood. In the centre of the room, looking out towards the sea, was a throne. Its back and one of its arms had long since broken off, but still it was plain to see what it was.

'Mia, can you pull my notebook from my pocket?' requested Jethro.

'J, we need to get our hands free first,' Lucy argued. 'Check the cupboards, Mia, please!'

Mia did as Lucy had requested and began to open the cupboards one by one. Some were empty, but she found six corked glass bottles in one, and a whole host of crockery in another. At length, she found a sharp knife with which she began carefully but quickly sawing away at Jethro's ropes. He was soon free, and then he was able to help everyone else.

Lucy winced as she rubbed her wrists, and then she decided to uncork one of the bottles, sniffing it cautiously. It smelt like luxury. She poured a little into a cup and took a sip. It was the most wonderful thing she had ever tasted: fruity, spicy and wonderfully warming, it spread delightfully through her whole being.

'Wow!' she said. 'I think this calls for a toast!' and she poured out a cup of the mysterious brew for each of them. 'Here's to our escape!' she said, handing the drinks round.

Everyone drained their cups and sighed contentedly. The liquid seemed to have great restorative powers, leaving them feeling altogether strong in body and sharp of mind.

'Look,' said Mia, 'the symbol on the bottle; it's the same as my ring!'

It was true: the glass was marked with the relief of the crown.

'Papa always joked that I was royalty, and now look, I have my very own bottles of drink!' she giggled softly.

'Actually,' said Lucy gently, 'your papa wasn't joking.'

Chapter twenty-three

Lucy explained to Mia what the King's brother had told them, about how he was actually related to Mia, and who she really was. Mia took the news in her stride. The revelations of royalty resonated with her already extraordinary experience of life. Being a princess was okay as long as she had her friends to help her, she reasoned. And Papa would always be her papa. It did not shock or upset her, much to Lucy and Jethro's relief. She was a very brave little girl – perfect princess material.

'Good. Now let's get this riddle solved,' Jethro announced, pulling his notebook out. 'The light's fading and it'll soon be evening. I wonder if they've missed us yet! Now listen up,' he ordered, and began to read. '"Complete the square, and the eye will no longer see: the desert will laugh, the throne will be true, hearts will unite, and eyes will be lit. Our enemy will scatter and fall away." What does anyone think?'

'"The miracle of the desert" – that must be what is referred to as the desert laughing, don't you think?' Lucy asked again. 'It's like I said – the Kingdom itself is on our side, longing for its freedom.'

'Yes, I agree,' said Jethro, 'so that's one thing. What else?'

'Not one thing,' Ella interjected. 'It's one side of the square! Don't you see? There are four sides: the desert, the throne, the hearts and the eyes.'

'Go on!' Jethro encouraged her excitedly.

'I don't know,' she said, 'I'll keep thinking. What about you, Luka?' she prompted. Her friend was shifting from one foot to the other, and she knew what that meant: he had something to say, but he was too shy to say it.

'Well, er,' he began hesitantly, 'for the throne to be true, it would need to have the true heir sitting on it, wouldn't it, and now we know who that is.'

'Luka, that's brilliant! Mia, come and sit on the throne!'

The little girl perched on the seat, dwarfed by its ungainly size. She crossed her legs and looked out towards the cave's mouth. 'I might have to grow into it,' she said meekly.

'Nonsense!' cried everyone in unison. They all felt in their hearts that she was a perfect fit.

'Look, on the floor in front of the throne, there's a square marked out!' Ella said suddenly. 'I was thinking it looked like someone had drawn the outline for a rug and then I realised it was a square!'

'It's like you said before, El,' Lucy said, remembering. 'We have to get them in the correct formation! Twins, you stand on either side of the throne and Jethro, place yourself opposite! Everyone put your toes on the line,' she suggested as an afterthought.

'But what about you?' Jethro asked.

'I'm only a visitor, J,' Lucy replied slowly.

'What? Lucy, you're as much a part of this Kingdom as us! You're part of its fabric, part of its folklore, part of me...' At this, his voice cracked a little.

'Thank you,' she said softly. 'You'll always be a part of me too. *This* will always be a part of me. But the future, here, it's for you and Mia, Zak and Luka. Now please, let yourself be organised by us!' she urged. 'Get around the square!'

'I need my cat!' Mia cried as everyone took their place. Lucy obediently collected him up and deposited him by her side.

'Now you have to hold hands!' Ella concluded. 'You can't hold hearts, but we all know that your hearts are united, so hold hands to symbolise it.'

Dutifully, the four friends clasped each other's hands, and then everyone waited. It was practically dark now.

Nothing happened. Everyone was holding their breath, expecting something to happen, anything, but it did not.

'Now what?' whispered Mia politely after a few moments had passed.

'Eyes will be lit?' Lucy proposed hopefully.

The four children let go of each other's hands and relaxed, trying to shrug off the tension.

Mia traced her finger idly along the arm of the throne until she found an indentation in the surface. It did not feel like a crack, and she leant in close to inspect it. It was a perfect circle with a crown in the centre. Curiously, she slipped her ring from her finger and pressed it with the crown face down into the hole.

Almost instantly, the air began to tremor and shake, and a noise like a loud trumpet rang in their ears.

Instinctively, Mia shouted above the clamour for everyone to get inside the square, and Lucy and Ella found themselves grabbed by friendly arms and pulled in close.

The noise soon ended, but the shaking carried on for a good few hours. It was most peculiar, for the ground was solid and stable, yet the air quaked, bombarded by wave after wave of energy and power, so that no one could move. It was not frightening. In fact, it was the very opposite, bringing absolute peace. They clung to one another as the waves moved through them and over them and about them. Lucy thought she could see the light changing around her, but it was not like sunrise. There was green and purple, now sparkling white. The coloured light on the walls kept changing, and it seemed to be growing brighter in the room.

Slowly but surely, the vibrations lessened until, at last, the children managed to crumple down to the floor. They had been standing, held up by the density of the air, so that they could not even sit. Everyone was too overwhelmed to speak for a very long time, until Mia broke the silence. 'Look,' she said simply, 'the light is back on.'

They followed her gaze towards the cave mouth. There outside was a powerful light, blinking on and off, on and off. The lighthouse was working again! Zak crawled over to take a look. His legs felt weak, and he was not sure he could remember how to walk. He stared out over the water. The great swarm of enemy ships was halfway out to sea and fleeing rapidly! The sky above was swirling with greens and purples and pinks, as if someone had scattered coloured dust across the night sky, and an enormous full moon shone bright.

'They've run away,' Zak reported, hardly believing his eyes. 'I think we've done it!'

As this news sank in, Lucy made a proposal. 'I'm going to get us a bottle, to celebrate.'

Though deeply drunk with peace, she somehow managed to get the cups and another bottle. Together they sat in a circle on the floor and drank to Mia and her Kingdom.

'This is a significant moment, J,' Lucy said. 'We must never forget it.'

'Never,' he agreed, touching his cup to hers.

The drink worked its magic once more, and though the peace stayed in their hearts, the strength returned to their legs, and they were alert and energetic once more.

'Shall I scout upstairs?' Zak offered.

'Yes, but be careful,' replied Jethro, though they all felt certain that the danger was gone, and for good.

Zak climbed back up the staircase, feeling his way slowly in the dark until he found the trapdoor blocking his way. He felt for the mechanism on the wall and tugged on it. The door opened downwards, and he climbed quickly up to the storeroom floor. It was just as they had left it, though there were no longer sounds of activity beyond the room. Investigating further, he found the door unlocked and, indeed, there was no one about. The place was absolutely abandoned, so he called back down the stairs. 'It's safe! Come on! Just watch the steps – that's all. It's a bit dark on the way up!'

Everyone came up out of the cavern into the lighthouse, and they hardly knew what to do with themselves. No doubt Captain Shaw would soon return for them when he realised what had happened. In the meantime, it was decided that they should have a meal together in the kitchen. While Lucy lit some candles, Jethro ran to get his pack of supplies from its hiding place outside. They also discovered more jars of dried fruit and spicy beans in the larder, and with Mia volunteering her bottles of drink, they all agreed that it was the best feast they had ever shared.

'There will be a feast every year on this day,' announced Mia. 'We will never forget what happened!'

Everyone laughed and toasted the princess. The meal went on long into the night, but the moon was still up when they had finished. Mia yawned deeply, and Lucy carried her upstairs and tucked her into one of the beds, with Nightfall curled up at her feet.

'Good night, Mia. Have a wonderful life,' she added, kissing her on the forehead. She began to feel heavy-hearted walking back downstairs, when she met Ella and Luka coming up.

'We're going to see the light,' Ella told her.

'Can I have a quick word, El? Do you mind, Luka?'

'No, of course not. I'll see you up there!' he said, trotting off up the steps.

'What is it, Lucy? You look sad; are you okay?'

'Yes, it's just that we might be going soon. You need to say goodbye properly – do you understand?'

Ella's face fell briefly, but then she smiled. Her eyes shone, probably from the tiniest beginning of tears. 'I understand,' she said. 'I'm just glad we got to help all the way to the end.'

'Yes, and you were amazing, little sister! Well, off you go and have fun!'

'I will!' called Ella, as she bounded off in search of her friend.

Lucy carried on slowly down the steps until she reached the sitting room. It was dark then light, dark then light as the lamp flashed rhythmically like the Kingdom's heartbeat. Glancing in, she saw Jethro sitting alone on a couch. He was staring out through the circular window, and he must have been lost in thought, because he did not hear her approach. She sat down next to him. Now she could see the moon shining yellow and low in the dark sky and over an even blacker sea. The reflection of pale golden light highlighted a portion of the waves. It was hauntingly beautiful.

'Has she settled?' he asked quietly.

'Yes, sound asleep,' Lucy confirmed.

They fell back into silence, and Lucy knew that Jethro had realised the same thing she had. Eventually, she reached her hand and placed it over his. She felt him tense ever so slightly, but she persevered. 'J, you're going to be alright,' she said.

He did not say anything and maintained his gaze out of the window.

'J, look at me!' she demanded.

He turned his countenance to her, and she tried to take in every detail before fixing her eyes to his. 'I want to memorise you, so that I'll never forget what you look like,' she said.

'Oh Lucy, how can you be so calm about this? I might never see you again! I want to see you every day,' he confessed.

'For a start, it's hard not to be calm when you've been microwaved by peace for hours on end! But that's not it. It's just that we have to cherish what we've had, not be ungrateful for what we can't have. You're usually the sensible one,' she added.

'I'm sorry. I'm not feeling sensible!' he replied petulantly, turning away from her and looking out the window once more.

She felt torn for him, and she desperately wanted to make it better, but only he could choose to let her go.

'The thing is, Jethro, our friendship is the dearest I've ever known, but I'm 100 per cent certain that you'll meet someone who will be perfect for you. Now that you understand what matters to you, you'll recognise her as soon as you meet her. And for now, you're going to be terribly busy helping Mia and the Duke. The Kingdom is without curse or enemy; that's something to be happy about!'

He was still quiet, but she noticed his shoulders relax, and finally he turned to her and smiled. 'I'm sorry,' he said. 'You're right, of course. I am grateful for all our time together and the new Kingdom – wow! Now is not a time for regrets, but I'm holding you to your word, that I will find someone to share it with!'

'I know you will,' she said, emphatically.

They sat together side by side as night began to fade towards dawn, and though they were both weary, neither dared sleep. A companionable silence settled in the room, leaving each to their own thoughts. The sky grew lighter by degrees and the early morning air grew cool, so they dragged a rug across their legs.

'Goodnight,' Lucy murmured, as she felt her eyes finally becoming too heavy to keep open. They both slept before the sun rose. It was going to be a glorious day, but not one that Lucy would wake to see.

Chapter twenty-four

When Lucy woke, she found herself fully dressed under her quilt. The clock said 9.30am. She felt oddly empty. Her adventure was over; she did not have two lives any more – only one. She held Jethro in her thoughts and wished him a life of love and adventure; nothing less would be worthy of him. Then she wondered about herself. What was her life destined to be like?

Just then, the bedroom door began to open and a pyjama-clad Ella walked in slowly. She looked older to Lucy, older than nine, with all the things she had experienced. Yet she was still happy to slip into her sister's bed and cuddle into her. 'The lamp was amazing,' she said. 'You should have come to see it. All the fragments of glass were fixed together, and you couldn't tell there had been even one crack. A silver mirror went round it, moving continuously and making it blink. We couldn't decide at all how it worked…'

'And how was Luka?' asked Lucy.

'Oh, he was happy! He's sure I'll get to come and visit again. *You* did, after all!'

'Maybe you will!' laughed Lucy. 'You are full of surprises, and you usually get your way once you're certain about something!'

'Exactly,' said Ella. 'In the meantime, I'm going to start a diary and write it all down.'

'I'd like to see that,' said Lucy, squeezing her, 'and if I'm ever mean to you again, El, just remind me how amazing you are!'

'I will,' laughed her sister.

'Now, I'd better have a shower. It's not the best, sleeping in your clothes!'

Ella disappeared off, and Lucy had the longest shower ever. Gallons of hot, steamy water poured over her head like a cascading, though pleasant, waterfall, and she felt all the kinks and weariness wash away.

As she re-entered her room, her mobile phone beeped. It must be a text message. She grabbed it, and seeing it was from Will, her heart raced a little. At least she only had one world now, so that should make things less complicated.

The text read, 'Fancy meeting for coffee? My turn to find out about you. W.'

Lucy towelled her hair and sat on her bed, wondering how she could explain who she was. If someone really wanted to know her, they would have to know about the whole dream adventure. If they wanted to understand what mattered to her, they would have to know everything.

Will was so different to Jethro, and yet she had already seen glimpses of how alike they were. A life of love and adventure – surely that was her destiny too. Without further hesitation, she picked up the phone and texted her reply, 'See you at two. Get ready for the roller coaster. L.'